学术顾问
(以姓氏笔画为序)

王 宏　冯智文　李正栓　李丽生　原一川

Academic Advisors
Wang Hong　Feng Zhiwen　Li Zhengshuan
Li Lisheng　Yuan Yichuan

主 编
李昌银

副主编
黄 瑛　彭庆华

General Editor
Li Changyin
Professor of English Yunnan Normal University

Associate General Editors
Huang Ying
Professor of English Yunnan Normal University
Peng Qinghua
Professor of English Yunnan Normal University

云南少数民族经典作品英译文库
Classics of Yunnan Ethnic Groups in English Translation

主编 李昌银　General Editor　Li Changyin
副主编 黄瑛　彭庆华　Associate General Editors　Huang Ying & Peng Qinghua

Old Folk Songs of the Dai & the Naxi
古 歌

搜集整理◎周良沛
英译◎陈金金
译校◎[美]包琼

Collected & Edited by Zhou Liangpei
Translated by Chen Jinjin
Revised by Joan Cecile Boulerice

云南出版集团
云南人民出版社

图书在版编目（CIP）数据

古歌：汉、英 / 周良沛搜集整理；陈金金英译
. -- 昆明：云南人民出版社，2018.12
（云南少数民族经典作品英译文库 / 李昌银主编）
ISBN 978-7-222-17499-3

Ⅰ.①古… Ⅱ.①周… ②陈… Ⅲ.①傣族—民间故事—中国—汉、英②纳西族—民间故事—中国—汉、英 Ⅳ.①I277.3

中国版本图书馆CIP数据核字(2018)第277437号

出 品 人	李　维　　赵石定
项目统筹	周　祥　　殷筱钊
项目组稿	郭木玉
责任编辑	郭木玉　　任建红　　李东华
设计制作	马　滨　　三人禾
责任校对	李智燕　　崔苡菡　　付芳侠　　周桉吉
责任印制	陆卫华　　代隆参

云南少数民族经典作品英译文库
Classics of Yunnan Ethnic Groups in English Translation

古 歌
Old Folk Songs of the Dai & the Naxi

搜集整理◎周良沛
英译◎陈金金
译校◎[美]包琼

Collected & Edited by Zhou Liangpei
Translated by Chen Jinjin
Revised by Joan Cecile Boulerice

出　版	云南出版集团　云南人民出版社
发　行	云南人民出版社
社　址	昆明市环城西路609号
邮　编	650034
网　址	www.ynpph.com.cn
E-mail	ynrms@sina.com
开　本	787mm×1092mm　1/16
印　张	16.75
字　数	240千
版　次	2018年12月第1版第1次印刷
印　刷	云南出版印刷（集团）有限责任公司　云南新华印刷一厂
书　号	ISBN 978-7-222-17499-3
定　价	95.00元

云南人民出版社
公众微信号

序 一

◎李正栓

  民族典籍英译是传播中国文化、文学和文明的重要途径，是中华文化走出去的重要组成部分。文化与文学的传播，是一个国家提高文化软实力的重要方式，在文化交流和文明建设中起着不可或缺的作用，对提高国家对外话语权、构建国家对外话语体系以及对建设世界文学都有积极意义。

  中国各少数民族拥有许多优秀的典籍，具有很高的文物价值、文学价值和文化价值。各民族的先人们通过口头流传或用文字记述了他们各具特色的文化。各少数民族几乎都有自己民族的创世史、史诗和神话传说。

  中国民族典籍独具特色，不可替代。重视民族典籍的翻译和研究工作，对于挖掘各民族优秀文化，保护各民族文明，增强各民族之间的沟通和了解，进一步向世界其他地区传播各少数民族优秀文化，乃至提高我国文化软实力都有着重要意义。不少少数民族聚居地处于祖国边疆，有的处在"一带一路"建设关键部位，有的处在与周边国家进行各种交流的重要位置。

  中国民族典籍是世界多元文化的有机组成部分，与其他文化共同造就了世界文化的绚丽多姿。世界正因为其文化多样性才变得缤纷多彩。我国各民族典籍中包含的文化多样性极大地丰富了世界多元、特色鲜明的文化。人们对多样性形成全新的认识角度和思维方式。多样性开阔了人们的视野，丰富了人们思考问题的角度。挖掘这些典籍中所蕴含的教育价值和文化价值，对世界其他民族都有指导和借鉴意义，并且有助于建设我国的文化自信。

民族典籍本身蕴含的特殊价值对加强民族文化了解、促进中外文化交流具有重大意义。民族典籍英译具有文学翻译和文化传递之功能，有对外宣传作用，还是一种文学外交。因此，民族典籍翻译和研究对于维护祖国统一、促进民族团结、稳定边疆以及增强国内各民族和中外文化之间的交流都起着极为重要的作用。

中华人民共和国成立以后，中央政府一直十分重视民族典籍翻译和研究工作，提供了强有力的政策支持，并采取了一系列有效措施，加快了各少数民族典籍的抢救、整理、翻译和研究的进程。中央政府多次召开西藏工作会议和新疆工作会议。近年来，国际和国内对于多元文化高度关注，少数民族文学典籍的翻译已然成为业内研究的热点。

近年来，民族典籍翻译和研究迅猛发展，势头良好。国家大力支持，发放国家社科基金课题，教育部和国家民委也发放课题，扶持了一大批研究者。很多民族典籍翻译课题得以立项并顺利开展；为数不少的民族典籍被翻译成汉语、英语和其他语言并出版发行；越来越多的业界人士致力于这个满富生机的学术领域。

在中国文化走出去的国家战略下，全国少数民族典籍英译学术研讨会陆续召开，已经召开三次。

云南是中国民族最多的省份。人口在5000人以上的少数民族有25个，其中有15个民族为云南所特有，分别是：白族、哈尼族、傣族、傈僳族、佤族、拉祜族、纳西族、景颇族、布朗族、普米族、阿昌族、基诺族、怒族、德昂族、独龙族。其中除白族人口占全国白族人口总数的84%以上外，其他14个民族95%居住在云南。

云南还是我国跨境民族最多的省份。在云南的25个少数民族中，有16个民族跨境而居，分别是：傣族、壮族、苗族、景颇族、瑶族、哈尼族、德昂族、佤族、拉祜族、彝族、阿昌族、傈僳族、布依族、怒族、布朗族、独龙族。

云南少数民族创造了辉煌的文化。据不完全统计，云南少数民族文字文献古籍蕴藏量达10万余册（卷），口传古籍4万余种。云南省民委少数民族古籍整理出版规划办公室为了挽救和保护这些古籍，计划在5年内编纂出版100卷《云南少数民族古籍珍本集成》。这是一个令人瞩目的庞大计划。将这些古籍中的珍品翻译介绍给世界，不仅能够弘扬云南省丰富多彩的民族文化，而且有助于增进与南亚东南亚国家的理解与交流，为"一带一路"倡议的实施做出贡献。

云南师范大学外国语学院很重视这一领域的工作。在外国语学院领导支持下，李昌银教授带领一个由教授和中青年学者组成的团队对精选出来的17部云南少数民族经典作品进行英译，计划在5年内（"十三五"期间）翻译出版。这是一项十分有意义的宏大工程。

这17部民族典籍，内容全部为各民族的英雄史诗或神话传说，具有很高的历史意义和文学价值。这些作品涉及阿昌族、白族、傣族、德昂族、哈尼族、景颇族、拉祜族、苗族、纳西族、普米族、彝族等11个少数民族。

  云南师范大学这支翻译队伍实力强大，主要由一些多年从事翻译教学、研究和实践的教授和副教授组成，他们是李昌银、黄瑛、彭庆华、孙兴文、吴相如、刘德周、杨慧芳、邰菊、陈萍、包琼（Joan Boulerice）等国内外专家学者。他们在云南翻译界都是风云人物。

  在民族典籍英译中，这支队伍异军突起，为我国民族典籍英译壮大了声势，必将为中国民族典籍走向世界而成为世界文学的一部分做出新贡献。

  民族典籍翻译与研究事业关乎国家的稳定统一，关乎民族关系的和谐发展，关乎世界多元文化的实现。在中国，民族典籍资源极为丰富，有待进一步挖掘、翻译。因此，民族典籍英译前景光明。同时，我们也应意识到，仍有许多濒临消失的少数民族典籍亟待拯救，民族典籍翻译与研究工作任重而道远。

  （李正栓，中国英汉语比较研究会典籍英译专业委员会常务副会长兼秘书长）

Foreword by Li Zhengshuan

The translation of Chinese ethnic classics is an important approach in spreading Chinese culture, literature and civilization. It is a crucial component of Chinese culture going global. The spreading of Chinese culture and literature is a national policy and an important way to improve the cultural soft power of China. It plays an indispensable role in the cultural exchange between China and other countries and the development of world literature.

The ethnic groups in China have countless excellent classics with high anthropological, literary and cultural value. The ancestors of each ethnic group have passed down their distinctive culture orally or in writing. Almost all the ethnic groups have their own story of creation, epics, myths and legends.

Chinese ethnic classics are unique and irreplaceable. It is imperative to attach importance to the translation and research of ethnic classics; to explore the excellent ethnic cultures; to protect the civilization of ethnic groups; to enhance the communication and understanding among ethnic groups; to further spread the outstanding culture of ethnic groups to other parts of the world; and to build the cultural strength of China. Many ethnic groups live in the border areas and thus play an important role in the cultural and economic cooperation between China and its neighbors in the context of the Belt and Road Initiative.

Chinese ethnic classics are an important component of the magnificence and diversity of world culture. It is diversity that makes the world so colorful. The cultural diversity of Chinese ethnic classics has greatly enriched the world's pluralism and its distinctive features. People around the world have formed a new understanding of diversity. This diversity has expanded people's horizon and enriched their way of thinking. Digging out the educational and cultural value in these classics can contribute to the construction of China's self-confidence in culture.

The special value of the ethnic classics itself is of great significance to the strengthening of national culture and intercultural communication between China and foreign countries. The translation of ethnic classics is not just a literary exchange, but also a form of cultural communication. It is diplomacy through literature in that it consolidates the cultural ties between China and other countries.

After the founding of the People's Republic of China, the central government attached great importance to the translation and research of ethnic classics, provided the a great deal of policy support, and adopted a series of effective measures to speed up the process of rescuing, collating, translating and studying ethnic classics. The central government has convened several working conferences on Tibet and Xinjiang. In recent years, both China and other countries have paid close attention to multiculture. The translation of ethnic classics has become a hot topic.

In recent years, the translation and research of ethnic classics have progressed rapidly and have shown good prospects. The government strongly supports and grants the research projects of the national social science fund. The Ministry of Education and the State Ethnic Affairs Commission are also issuing research projects and giving funding to a large number of researchers. Many research projects on ethnic classics have been approved and carried out. Many ethnic classics have been translated into Chinese, English and other languages and published. More and more professionals have dedicated themselves to this new sphere of learning.

In this context, the academic conferences on translation of ethnic classics are held one after another all around the country. And up to now three have been held.

Yunnan is the province which has the most ethnic groups in China. Besides Han people, there are 25 ethnic groups, each with a population of more than 5,000. Among them, 15 ethnic groups are unique to Yunnan, which are the Bai, the Hani, the Dai, the Lisu, the Wa, the Lahu, the Naxi, the Jingpo, the Bulang, the Pumi, the Achang, the Jinuo, the Nu, the De'ang and the Dulong. Among these, 84% of the total number of the Bai people in China and 95% of the other 14 ethnic groups are living in Yunnan.

Yunnan is also the province which has the most cross-border ethnic groups. Of the 25 ethnic groups, 16 live across the border, namely: the Dai, the Zhuang, the Miao, the Jingpo, the Yao, the Hani, the De'ang, the Wa, the Lahu, the Yi, the Achang, the Lisu, the Buyi, the Nu, the Bulang and the Dulong.

The ethnic groups in Yunnan have created splendid cultures. According to statistics, the number of classics of Yunnan ethnic groups is more than 100 thousand volumes and classics in oral tradition are more than 40 thousand. In order to save and protect these ancient books, the Office of Classics Collation and Publishing of Yunnan Ethnic Groups Affairs Commission planned to compile and publish 100 volumes of *A Collection of Yunnan Ethnic Group Rare Books* in five years, which is an ambitious plan. The introduction of the ancient classics via translation can not only promote and develop the colorful ethnic cultures of Yunnan, but also contribute to the understanding and exchange between China and countries in South Asia and Southeast Asia and to the implementation of the Belt and Road Initiative as well.

The School of Foreign Languages and Literature of Yunnan Normal University is paying close attention to this field. With the support of the School and the University, Professor Li Changyin is leading a group of professors and young scholars to do the project of *"Classics of Yunnan Ethnic Groups in English Translation"*, which includes 17 ethnic classics selected carefully from Yunnan's bountiful ethnic classics. These books are the heroic epics or myths and legends of each ethnic groups with great historical significance and literary value. They will finish the translation in five years (during "the thirteenth five-year plan"). After that, all the works will be published by Yunnan People's Publishing House.

The 17 works cover 11 ethnic groups: the Achang, the Bai, the Dai, the De'ang, the Hani, the Jingpo, the Lahu, the Miao, the Naxi, the Pumi and the Yi. All of these groups except the Miao and the Yi are unique to Yunnan.

The translation team of Yunnan Normal University is full of strength and vitality, composed of professors and associate professors who have been occupied in translation teaching, research, and practice for a long time. They are Li Changyin, Huang Ying, Peng Qinghua, Sun Xingwen, Wu Xiangru, Liu Dezhou, Yang Huifang, Gao Ju, Chen Ping, Joan Boulerice and other experts and scholars who are representative figures in the translation field in Yunnan province.

This team is a new force that has suddenly arisen in terms of translating ethnic classics. It is expanding the momentum of ethnic classics translation in China and has made a new contribution for China's ethnic classics to go global and become a part of world literature.

The translation and research of ethnic classics are related

to the development of Chinese culture and the realization of multiculturalism in the world. In China, ethnic classics are extremely rich in resources, which require us to make further exploration and research and translate them into other languages. Therefore, the future of translating ethnic classics is bright. At the same time, we should also realize that there are still many ethnic works which are close to extinction and urgently need to be rescued. We still have a long way to go in the fields of translation and research in ethnic classics.

(Li Zhengshuan, Standing Vice Chairman and Secretary General, Classics Translation Committee of CACSEC)

序 二

◎王 宏

好友云南师范大学外国语学院李昌银教授来电嘱托我为"云南少数民族经典作品英译文库"的出版写一序言,并随即发来该文库的背景资料,让我"不着急,慢慢写"。我本人从事中国典籍英译及研究,深知少数民族典籍对外传译的重要性,但又是少数民族典籍翻译的门外汉。因此,我是怀着虚心学习的态度来写此序言的。近年来,在中国文化"走出去"战略工程大背景下,在中央和地方各级政府的大力支持下,我国少数民族典籍的对外传译及研究工作顺利开展,取得了很大的进步。请看以下数据:

2008年,广西百色学院韩家权教授获批国家社科基金项目《布洛陀史诗》(壮汉英对照)。该项目已顺利结项,并于2013年12月获得中国民间文艺最高奖"山花奖"。

2012年,广西百色学院外语系翻译团队翻译的国家级非物质文化遗产《壮族嘹歌》(英文版)由广西师范大学出版社正式出版。

2012年,东北大学秦皇岛分校吴松林教授主编的《蒙古族系列:江格尔(汉英对照)》(上下册)由吉林大学出版社出版。

2013年,河北师范大学李正栓教授英译《藏族格言诗》

由长春出版社出版发行。

2013年，云南财经大学崔晓霞教授撰写的《〈阿诗玛〉英译研究》收入由王宏印教授主编、民族出版社出版的"民族典籍翻译研究丛书"。

2014年，东北大学秦皇岛分校吴松林教授撰写的《满族档案文献研究》申请到国家社科后期资助，他英译的《英雄格斯尔可汗》由吉林大学出版社出版。

2014年，中南民族大学张立玉教授主持的"土家族主要典籍英译及研究"获批国家社科基金项目。

2015年，西安外国语大学梁真惠副教授撰写的《〈玛纳斯〉翻译传播研究》收入由王宏印教授主编、民族出版社出版的"民族典籍翻译研究丛书"。

与此同时，第一届和第二届全国少数民族典籍英译学术研讨会分别于2012年和2014年在广西民族大学和大连民族学院举行，参加会议的院校分布之广、与会代表数量之众、提交论文数量之多和涉及研究话题之细，十分可喜。2016年还将在中南民族大学举行第三届全国少数民族典籍英译学术研讨会。

为什么少数民族典籍的对外传译及研究工作在短短几年就受到译界的青睐，取得众多成果？我认为，这在很大程度上归于典籍翻译界乃至翻译界同仁对"中国典籍"的重新思考和认识。中国典籍浩如烟海，卷帙浩繁，举世瞩目，是全人类共同的精神财富。但对于中国典籍的理解，我们以前较多限于汉民族的重要文献和书籍，而对少数民族多有忽略。在讨论中国典籍时，也较多关注古代文学作品。其实，中国典籍指"中国清代末年1911年以前的重要文献和书籍",这就要求我们从事典籍翻译时,不但要翻译古代文学典籍作品,还要翻译古代哲学、科技、法律、医学、经济、军事、天文、地理等诸多方面的典籍作品,不但要翻译汉民族的典籍作品,也要翻译各少数民族的典籍作品。

民族典籍具有该民族的原型符号的特质,蕴藏着能够"遗传"并不断"再生"的文化基因。民族典籍是中华传统文化的内核,同时还是中华传统文化的符号构成规则。中国是具有56个民族的多民族国家,少数民族典籍是我国少数民族勤劳与智慧的结晶,是中华文明、也是世界文明不可或缺的一部分。少数民族典籍对外传译具有跨文化交流的作用,它不但有助于更多的人了解少数民族的独特文化,而且还有助于保护少数民族文化的独特性、维持少数民族文化多样性、促进各民族团结、提升中华文化软实力等。

中国少数民族典籍涉及宗教、文学、历史、语言、医学、天文历算等领域,内容丰富,版本多样,载体特殊,传承奇特。仅以《中国少数民族古籍总目提要》为例,该书于1997年正式立项,全书总体设计约60卷、110册,目前已出版23个民族卷共20册:纳西族卷、白族卷、东乡族卷·裕固族卷·保安族卷、土族卷·撒拉族卷、锡伯族卷、哈尼族卷、回族卷·铭刻、柯尔克孜族卷、羌族卷、毛南族卷·京族卷、仫佬族卷、达斡尔族卷、土家族卷、鄂温克族卷、鄂伦春族卷、赫哲族卷、苗族卷、侗族卷、黎族卷、朝鲜族卷。该书真实地反映了我国各少数民族古籍赋存的全面情况,充实了中国的历史和文化内容,为后人探索各种文化形式的源流、揭示中国社会文化发展的轨迹提供了极为珍贵的资料,为我国乃至世界各国人文科学研究提供了一套新颖而全面的资料,对于弘扬中华民族传统文化具有深远的历史意义和现实意义。

少数民族典籍的对外传译是一项艰巨的工作,涉及将少数民族语言译成汉语、少数民族语言之间的互译和少数民族语言译成外语(主要是英语)。前两类翻译历史源远流长,最早可追溯到春秋战国时代《越人歌》的翻译,即汉、壮语之间的翻译。少数民族典籍译成外语的时间则要晚一些。据考证,维吾尔族古典长诗《福乐智慧》成书于1069年或1070年,目前尚未发现完整的原稿,只存留下来三个抄本,分别为赫拉特抄本、费尔干纳抄本与埃及抄本,其中费尔干纳抄本于12~13世纪用阿拉伯文纳斯赫体抄写,1914年发现于今中亚乌孜别克斯坦纳曼干城,现存于该共和国科学院东方研究所。这是少数民族典籍译介到国外的最早纪录。少数民族典籍外译在现代有了较快发展。一些少数民族典籍,如藏族的《格萨尔王传》、蒙古族的《江格尔》和柯尔克孜族的《玛纳斯》等英雄史诗,云南彝族的《阿诗玛》、维吾尔族的《艾里甫和赛乃姆》等民间叙事长诗已先后被翻译成英语及其他外国文字,为世人所知。这对传承少数民族经典,推动中外文化交流起到了不可替代的作用。然而,还有大量的中国少数民族典籍等待我们去翻译和研究。

云南省少数民族典籍资源十分丰富。据不完全统计,云南少数民族文字文献古籍蕴藏量达10万余册(卷),口传古籍4万余种。"云南少数民族经典作品英译文库"正是依托云南省丰富的少数民族典籍资源,借助云南师范大学外国语学院强大的翻译师资队伍，在云南人民出版社的有力支持下，首次将云南少数民族经典作品成系列对外译介的大力举措。云南师范大学外国语学院对"云南少数民族经典作品英译文库"十分重视，他们首先邀请省内外少数民族语言文化研究专家对云南民族典籍和民族文化经典作品进行筛选，做到"好中选好，优中选优"，同时调配最强的翻译力量承担文库的翻译任务。我粗略看了该文库的选题，发现选题面广，覆盖范围宽，收入了云南省阿昌族、白族、傣族、纳西族、德昂族、哈尼族、景颇族、拉祜族、苗族、普米族和彝族等民族的典籍作品。云南共有25个少数民族，其中11个少数民族的典籍作品都覆盖到了，不少作品还是首次译成英文。这将彻底改变云南少数民族典籍由于对外译介数量较少，不为世界了解的尴尬局面。

对于云南师范大学外国语学院而言，把少数民族典籍英译作为翻译专业的优势特色进行建设，这将对该院的学科建设起到助推作用。"云南少数民族经典作品英译文库"所产生的翻译成果和研究成果将培养出一批优秀的典籍翻译和研究团队，凸显该院在全国的学术特色和学术影响，同时还能将翻译能力和研究能力转化为教学能力，提高云南师范大学外国语学院翻译专业研究生的培养质量，为社会输送高水平的翻译人才，有力地支撑学院翻译专业学科的建设和发展。我对云南师范大学外国语学院的翻译师资队伍较为熟悉。作为云南省唯一获得省级高校优势特色学科建设项目的外国语学院，该院具有雄厚的翻译师资力量，在云南省各高校中当属第一。多年来，该院翻译与跨文化研究团队一直承担着对外交流与合作的各种口笔译项目及任务。由外国语学院精心挑选和确定的"云南少数民族经典作品英译文库"翻译人员绝大多数都是云南省翻译领域里的知名教授或专家，有国外留学经历，且具有扎实的英汉双语语言功底，曾翻译出版多部译著和翻译作品，并且主持和参与过多项翻译项目的研究。我阅读李昌银教授发来的文库翻译人员名单，发现多名我所熟悉的知名教授、博士也在其中，感到格外放心。

"云南少数民族经典作品英译文库"的出版发行是云南省翻译界的一件大事，也是我国少数民族典籍翻译传来的又一佳音。想当年，我和《大中华文库》总协调人李林老师曾在参加全国典籍英译学术研讨会之余一起找到李昌银教授，敦促李教授向学校和同事呼吁，少数民族典籍翻译及研究是富矿，值得快挖、深挖，能早出成果，出大成果。今天，我们当年的心愿变成了美好的现实，心里感到特别高兴。再次热烈祝贺"云南少数民族经典作品英译文库"的顺利出版！

（王宏，中国典籍翻译研究会副会长、苏州大学博士生导师）

Foreword by Wang Hong

My friend Professor Li Changyin of Yunnan Normal University asked me to write a few words for the publication of *Classics of Yunnan Ethnic Groups in English Translation*. I am more than delighted to do it. As I have been doing research in the English translation of Chinese classics, I know how important his work is. In recent years, substantial progress has been made in translating Chinese ethnic classics into English and other foreign languages. Books published in this respect include *The Liao Songs of the Zhuang Nationality* (Nanning: Guangxi Normal University Press, 2008, English Edition), *Mongolian Series: Jianggeer* (Changchun: Jilin University Press, 2012, Bilingual Edition), *Tibetan Gnomic Verses Translated into English* (Changchun: Changchun Press, 2013), and *Geser Khan: a Hero* (Changchun: Jilin University Press, 2014). Several projects in the English translation of ethnic classics have received funding from the National Planning Office of Philosophy and Social Science and, as a result, a number of monographs and PhD dissertations have been published.

Meanwhile, it is encouraging to see that the first conferences on English translation of ethnic classics in China have been held in Guangxi Nationalities University and

Dalian Nationalities Institute respectively. Participants were both many and enthusiastic. Many papers were presented and a lot of topics discussed. The third conference will be hosted by South Central Nationalities University in 2016.

Why, then, has this field attracted so much attention from translators and scholars alike and accomplished so much in just a few years? The answer, I believe, lies in a rethinking of what constitutes Chinese classics as an indispensable part of human heritage. We used to see Chinese classics as more or less equal to the classics of the Han people, excluding works by other ethnic groups. Moreover, when we talk about Chinese classics, we focus too much on the literary works of ancient times. Yet Chinese classics actually refer to "important works and books before 1911, the year when the Qing dynasty fell, bringing an end to imperial rule." This definition requires us to pay attention not just to literary works, but also writings in other subjects, such as philosophy, science, law, medicine, economics, military affairs, astronomy, and geography, not only Han works, but writings by other ethnic groups as well.

The classical works of a nation are its archetypal symbols, the major carriers of its cultural genes. Chinese classics make up the core of Chinese tradition. The Chinese nation consists of 56 ethnic groups. Ethnic classics are an important part of not only Chinese traditional culture, but also of world civilization. The translation of these works into other languages is important in that it helps to promote cross-cultural communications between China and other countries and to protect and preserve the uniqueness and diversity of ethnic cultures by making them accessible to foreign readers.

Chinese ethnic classics cover a variety of areas, such as religion, literature, history, language, medicine, astrology, and calendar, with numerous editions, special media and unique ways of transmission from generation to generation. Take, for example, *An Anthology of Chinese Ethnic Classics*, a colossal project that includes 110 volumes, 20 of which, from 23 ethnic groups, have been published. The anthology reflects the variety and quantity of China's ethnic classics and provides valuable material and resources for studying, understanding and developing Chinese culture and history in a more comprehensive and sustainable way.

The translation of Chinese ethnic classics into foreign languages is a very demanding job, involving rendering from ethnic languages to Chinese, between ethnic languages, and from ethnic languages (often via Chinese) to foreign languages. The first two types of translation can be traced back to the Spring and Autumn Period, when *The Song of the Yue People* was translated from their mother tongue into Chinese. The earliest translation of ethnic classics into a foreign language is *Wisdom of Royal Glory*, a long poem of the Uygurs, which was rendered from the source language into Arabic and is now in the Oriental Institute of Uzbekistan at Namangan. But it was not until modern times that the translation of ethnic classics into foreign languages accelerated. Noticeably, ethnic epics, such as *The Story of Prince Geser* of the Tibetans, *The Story of Jianggeer* of the Mongolians, *Manas* of the Kyrgyz, and narrative poems such as *Ashima* of the Yi people, *Alip and Salam* of the Uygurs, etc., have been published. These translations have contributed to acquainting the world with Chinese ethnic classics, but many remain to be translated.

Yunnan is rich in ethnic classics, boasting more than 100 thousand volumes of written classics and over 40 thousand pieces of oral literature. Relying on such bountiful resources, as a collective endeavor of the translation team of the School of Foreign Languages and Literature, Yunnan Normal University and with the help of Yunnan People's Publishing House, *Classics of Yunnan Ethnic Groups in English Translation* is the first project to translate Yunnan ethnic classics into English on a large scale. The School adheres to a professional spirit and academic standard in carrying out the project by selecting the most authoritative texts in the source language (Chinese) and recruiting the best translators from its huge faculty. The selection of the works, covering eleven of the twenty-five ethnic groups of the province, indicates expertise and insight. The implementation of the project will change the embarrassing obscurity of Yunnan ethnic classics by making them known to the world, many of them for the first time.

In light of disciplinary development, the project is of

great importance, too. Participating in the translation will strengthen the academic foundation of the teachers, enrich their experience and enhance their translation skills and research ability. This in turn will help them become better teachers and thus able to educate students with higher quality. The publication of the books will add greatly to the faculty accomplishments of the School and raise the academic standing of Yunnan Normal University by taking the first step in this direction among the universities of Yunnan province.

This publication project is a great event not only for Yunnan itself, but also for China. Looking back, I remember that Professor Li Changyin, our friend Li Lin, editor of the *Library of Chinese Classics*, and I talked enthusiastically about initiating something like this in Yunnan when we attended a conference on the translation of ethnic classics in Soochow. Lin and I strongly suggested that Professor Li do it as soon as possible. Now I am very pleased to see our talk becoming reality. Again, my congratulations on the publication of *Classics of Yunnan Ethnic Groups in English Translation*!

(Wang Hong, PhD supervisor at Soochow University, Vice Chairman of Classics Translation Committee of CACSEC)

General Introduction

This publication project, Classics of *Yunnan Ethnic Groups in English Translation*, aims at introducing Yunnan ethnic classical works to the world by making them available to native speakers of English who might be interested in them. With the publication of the *Library of Chinese Classics*, which consists only of books written by Han authors in classical Chinese, attention now is being turned to the English translation and publication of ethnic classics, books produced by ethnic writers about their history and culture. Universities in provinces such as Guangxi, Guizhou, Liaoning, Xinjiang, and Xizang, have taken the initiative. We in Yunnan must do something, because Yunnan has the largest number of ethnic groups in China. 15 of the 25 ethnic groups in the province, the Bai, the Dai, the Hani, the Lisu, the Wa, the Lahu, the Naxi, the Jingpo, the Bulang, the Pumi, the Achang, the Jinuo, the Nu, the De'ang, and the Dulong, live in no other place but Yunnan. The classics of these people, either in their own languages or in Chinese translations, are a great treasure house, which should be accessible to English readers and scholars. But what works should be translated first?

All the 25 ethnic groups in Yunnan have their classics, epics, mythology, creation stories, folksongs, folk drama, mountain songs, and funeral lament lyrics, most of which exist in different versions in different places. According to one estimation, there are more than 100 thousand volumes of them, excluding those in oral form. After a thorough survey and extensive consultations with experts of ethnic studies, we concluded that priority must be given to epics and mythologies, as they reflect an ethnic people's philosophy, history and culture more than anything else by narrating the stories of where and how they think they came from. From many epics and mythologies, we selected 17 of the most authoritative and popular classics representing 11 Yunnan ethnic groups, the Yi, the Bai, the Miao, the Hani, the Lahu, the Naxi, the Jingpo, the Pumi, the Achang, the Dai, and the De'ang. These works are all in Chinese, translated from the original by bilingual scholars whose mother tongue is their own ethnic language and who are fluent and proficient in Chinese. Some were recorded from their oral form at rituals and performances. We did not choose texts written in the ethnic language, not least because it is very hard to find a translator who is skilled in both the ethnic language and English. Moreover, some of the classics in the ethnic language were circulated in various oral forms and fragments. The published Chinese versions have been carefully edited and translated, hence they are more reliable. The next question is: how to translate them?

It happens that all of the 17 works except one are in

verse form, with lines more or less the same length and loose rhymes, but no regular meter. A poem must be rendered into a poem; anything less is unacceptable. So here are the general rules we follow when doing the translation.

One. If the original is verse, the translated text must be verse, too.

Two. Reproduce the ideas and the images of the original as completely as possible.

Three. Reproduce the figures of speech of the original as much as possible.

Four. Do not change the number of lines in a stanza unless absolutely necessary.

Five. Do not use standard meters in English, because the Chinese original does not follow any regular meter. Use the natural rhythm of English instead, but most of the lines should look more or less the same length.

Six. Do not use rhyme unless it comes naturally and is faithful to the content of the original.

What we try to do is, to use Susan Bassnett's words, "transplant the seed", not the tree itself. As for the various aspects of form, particularly meter and end rhyme, we reproduce them when it is possible and abandon them when it is necessary.

Who will do the translations? As this is a collective project of the School of Foreign Languages and Literature of Yunnan Normal University, our team consists of a dozen faculty members and two students from our MA translation program who are already teachers in other universities. All the translators have been teaching translation and doing translation research for a long time. They have published not just academic articles on translation, but also translated books from English to Chinese or vice versa.

Traditionally, people translate into their mother tongue, not into a foreign language. But the situation is changing. Many translators today are translating from their mother tongue into a foreign language. The quality can be good, as Nike K. Pokorn and Stuart Campbell prove in *Challenging the Traditional Axioms*: *Translation into a non-mother tongue* (Amsterdam: John Benjamins Publishing Company, 2005) and *Translation into the Second Language* (New York: Routledge, 2013) respectively. The case of China provides further evidence for their argument. The translation of Chinese classics into English was initiated by James Legge and Herbert Allen Giles in the 19th century and carried on in the 20th century by Arthur Waley, David Hawkes, Burton Watson, John Minford, Stephen Owen and others. It is noticeable that these English and American sinologists were soon joined by Chinese scholars residing in the West, such as Hongming (Tomson) Gu and Lin Yutang, among others. They took up the job because they thought it was their obligation to give English readers more faithful translations than Western sinologists could, who, as their target language is their mother tongue, often misinterpret the original text and misrepresent Chinese culture. Since the 1950s, there has been an increasingly powerful trend for Mainland Chinese translators to render or re-render Chinese classics into foreign languages, English in particular. In our time, this work is gathering momentum, enthusiastically advocated and actively practiced by such well-known translation experts as Yang Xianyi of Beijing Foreign Language Press, Xu Yuanchong of Beijing University, Wang Rongpei of Dalian Foreign Language Institute, Wang Hongyin of Nankai University, Wang Hong of Soochow University, Li Zhengshuan of Hebei Normal University, and many more. These professors are not just translators, but also scholars in translation studies. More importantly, some of them, Xu Yuanchong, Wang Hong and Li Zhengshuan, for example, have had their translations published by Western publishers, which suggests that their English meets the international standard.

In the case of our project, we request that the translators do their best to produce good translations. When they submit them to us, they should represent the highest level that they can attain. Then the general editors appointed by the School read the translated texts and remove inaccurate renderings and grammar mistakes if there are any. On top of that, we've taken an indispensable measure to ensure that our English is readable. We asked Ms. Joan Cecile Boulerice, an American teacher who has been teaching English in our school since

2009, to read every text that we've translated and improve the English by making it more natural and idiomatic. This is the best we can do. Of course any problems that still remain in the translations are ours. They have nothing to do with our American teacher.

As the project is well under way, we would like to thank all those who have helped to make it possible. Ms Guo Muyu, director of the South and Southeast Asia Editorial Department, Yunnan People's Publishing House, has been most helpful in our cooperation. In addition, she has added importance to the project by turning it into a national publication project. Yunnan Normal University has supported us by paying the publication fees so that the translators won't have to be burdened with the financial responsibilities for this project. Professor Li Zhengshuan and Professor Wang Hong not only have always encouraged us to go on but have also written the forewords for the project, putting it in a global perspective. Ms Joan Boulerice's revision has ensured the fluency of the translated texts. Finally, special thanks must be given to Professor Wang Hong, again, and Mr Li Lin of Hunan People's Press for their suggestion that has helped us conceive the project from the very beginning.

(The General Editors, School of Foreign Languages & Literature, Yunnan Normal University, Kunming)

A Brief Introduction to
Old Folk Songs of the Dai & the Naxi

As a book of the Yunnan Ethnic Folklore Classics, *Old Folk Songs of the Dai & the Naxi* includes ten folk songs of the Dai and the Naxi. Back in 1956, Zhou Liangpei gathered some Dai folk songs and later published them as *Old Folk Songs of the Dai*. It was less than fifty pages, covering themes of love and marriage, house building, war and migration. Half a century later, Zhou incorporated three Naxi folk songs in the book and republished them as *Old Folk Songs of the Dai & the Naxi* in 2010. The three Naxi folk songs are: *Wusami of Dale*, *Sad Wandering Song*, and *Hunting Song*.

Old songs are folk tales popular among the ethnic groups in south China. They tell the myths and legends of the creation of the world as imagined by the ancestors of these people. While collecting the songs, Zhou first invited Zanha, local professional singers, to sing, but later he asked some minority university students who could sing to come and help. Those students were not only proficient in their own minority languages but also had learned Mandarin Chinese. So songs recorded were closer to their originals and became important materials for study of the folk literature and culture of the Dai and the Naxi.

The Translator

古歌 | 目录

古老的傣歌 // 1
路　遇 // 2

婚　歌 // 14

一朵菊花 // 20

怨　歌 // 40

传　歌 // 54

战　歌 // 58

盖　屋 // 64

纳西古歌三首 // 77
达勒·乌萨米 // 78

猎　歌 // 140

游　悲 // 182

Contents

Old Folk Songs of the Dai // 1

Sweet Encountering // 3

Wedding Song // 15

Song of a Chrysanthemum // 21

Sad Song about Love // 41

Song of a Legend // 55

Song of War // 59

House Building Song // 65

Three Old Folk Songs of the Naxi // 77

Wusami of Dale // 79

Hunting Song // 141

Sad Wandering Song // 183

古老的傣歌
Old Folk Songs of the Dai

路　遇

男：
我们又在这里相遇，
姑娘，你家在什么地方？

女：
我的家在不远不近的村庄，
哥哥，哪里又是你的家乡？

男：
我家叫满当垫满哦，
是一个自由的村庄。

姐姐，我的口里淡淡的，
你是否带来果子，给我尝尝？

女：
果子，我没有带来，
只有果林的花儿正开。

Sweet Encountering

Male:

Heaven again lets us meet here,

Maiden, where are you from?

Female:

I am from a village, so close, yet so far from here,

Brother, where are you from then?

Male:

I live in Mandangdianman

Where people believe in freedom.

Sister dear, do you bring any fruits?

Inside my mouth is tasteless.

Female:

No would be my answer,

Yet fruit trees are in full bloom.

男：

你不能给我果味尝，

那就给我一朵花吧，插在衣襟上。

女：

我真想送你一朵花，

可是无数朵，不知你爱哪一个她？

男：

好多花，我不看在心上，

只有一朵，开在我的身旁。

女：

哪朵花是开在你身旁，

你想她，可又怎么想？

男：

芭蕉熟了吊在树上，

孩子想要天上的月亮。

女：

哥哥，月亮圆圆的才好，

你为什么爱它缺了一方？

Old Folk Songs of the Dai

Male:

Pick me a blossom then

For the decoration of my clothes.

Female:

Among countless blossoms, I wonder,

Which one do you favor over others?

Male:

Only one in full bloom beside me

Has stolen my heart already.

Female:

How can I not see the one beside you?

How much, if so, are you missing her?

Male:

On the tree hang ripened bananas,

Just like the moon children crave for.

Female:

Brother dear, adorable is the full moon,

Why do you instead love the waning one?

哎，我不知道你在怎么想，
是不是已经爱上十五的月亮？

男：
十五的月亮曾滑过我头上，
我单单爱月儿缺了一方。

假若我昧着心爱上了她，
铜巴①里，你怎么不见我把她装上？

倒是你像鹦鹉一样满天飞，
不知哪个猎人，拿到你的翅膀？

女：
不，我不像鹦鹉满天飞舞，
我是孤独的若肖②，不出门一步。

除了母亲，我没见过外人，
我爱谁？你是我看见的第一个男人！

男：
是啰，过去有人说：

---
① 铜巴：傣族人用的织花口袋。
② 若肖：傣语，一种野鸟，白天不飞出来。

古老的傣歌
Old Folk Songs of the Dai

Alas, I know not what you are dwelling on,
Perhaps the full moon is what you are fond of.

Male:

Not a glimpse at the full moon when it showed up,
The one with imperfection is my love.

Lies if I told and fell for the full moon,
In my Tongba① why should I not put it?

Unlike you, living as a parrot flying freely in the sky,
Which lucky hunter, I wonder, can have your wings?

Female:

The parrot is what I resemble least, instead, I am
The lonely Ruoxiao② staying at home all day.

Who should I fall in love with? Brother dear,
You are the very first man I have ever met!

Male:

Fair maiden, I once heard:

---
① Tongba: a bag with woven patterns used by the Dai.
② Ruoxiao: Dai language referring to a wild bird which stays inside in the daytime.

"是神决定的,我们相遇在这条小路。"

那你有什么话都对我说了吧!
你看到的第一个男人,是否能做你的丈夫?

女:
若上天已定我们的姻缘,
终有一天,我们会在一起;

哥哥,日子还长得很哩,
你又何必太急!

我俩的姻缘还像根信梅波①,
要牢,要成粗线,还得用力搓。

只要你不忘记我,
我会记住你啊,哥哥!

男:
我爱你爱在心底,
可是又没东西送给你——

世上会有这样的女人,

---

① 信梅波:傣族搓灯芯的一种细线,容易断。

Old Folk Songs of the Dai

"Pure destiny allows us to meet here."

What is buried deep in your heart, please pour out to me!
Would you accept the man you first met to be your lifelong love?

Female:

If we are destined to stay together,
We will be one day, I believe;

Brother dear, we just met today,
Why are you so rushed to make promises?

What connects us now resembles a vulnerable Xinmeibo①,
To make it stronger we must twist harder.

Brother dear, forever I shall remember you,
Only if you never let go of me from your heart!

Male:

I love you from the bottom of my heart,
Yet have nothing to present to you.

How would it be possible to catch your heart

---

① Xinmeibo: a thin thread (easily broken) used for twisting the lamp wick by the Dai.

不用什么也能拴住她的心？

唉，我真怕你三心二意，
弄得我也心神不定……

女：
只要你对我说真话我就爱你，
我给你个铜钮①作个订婚礼；

它一面可作我俩结婚的被面闪闪发光，
它一面可作枕头，我俩好枕在花缎上。

男：
一心想伸手接过铜钮，
男人家在这时也脸红、害羞；

我像看到饭，当我饥饿，
伸出手去，你交给我！

女：
哥哥，希望你也给我一个你心爱之物，
你又给我什么？

---

① 铜钮：一种古老的铜巴，可以吊在腰上。

古老的傣歌
Old Folk Songs of the Dai

Without anything special to prove?

Alas, the thing that disturbs my mind
Is whether your heart will be faithful to me…

Female:
My heart belongs solely to you if you are honest to me,
A Tongniu① I present to you as an engagement gift;

One side glitters like our wedding quilts,
And the flip side the satin pillow we sleep on.

Male:
Were it not for my shyness,
Right away I would take it;

O what I feel right now is like
Food you give me when I am starving!

Female:
Brother dear, what is your precious gift
Given to me to prove your love?

---

① Tongniu: an ancient Tongba which can be hung at the waist.

男：
你哥哥出门来不及带东西，
只带了一个装烟的小盒盒；

用它和你订婚最合适，
它每时每刻都跟着我！

鄂圭① 过去就是十二月，
把你娶过来，可好啰！②

---
① 鄂圭：傣族一个节日。
② 下面还有十二行，意思与前面相同，故删去。

古老的傣歌
Old Folk Songs of the Dai

Male:

In a hurry was I this morning,

Only a tobacco box did I take along with me;

Yet all along I bring it with me,

A perfect engagement gift is it for you!

December[1] approaches right after the Egui[2] Festival,

How about I marry you then, my love?[3]

---

[1] The months in the Dai songs refer to lunar months in the Dai calendar. —Translator's note
[2] Egui: a festival of the Dai.
[3] The following twelve lines were deleted due to repetition.

婚　歌

暮色苍茫的黄昏，
小姑娘走出了树林；
背一捆干柴回寨来，
把坪地打扫干净。

烧起火塘纺线子，
等待小伙子来串门；
凳子不够有笓棚①，
笓棚不够地上蹲。

年纪大的不留他：
"这里没有你的份！"
年纪轻的对他说：
"请坐请坐，谈谈心！"

小伙子对小姑娘说：
"我不敢多耽搁，

---
① 笓棚是傣族家用的竹篾编成的矮凳。

古老的傣歌
Old Folk Songs of the Dai

Wedding Song

At the hazy dusk of twilight,
Out of the woods came a lovely maiden;
After collecting some firewood for home,
She began to do some sweeping.

While spinning beside the fire pit,
She was expecting some lad to come around;
Bipeng① were prepared in case of running short of stools,
And sit on your heels if there was no Bipeng left.

Unwelcome to the seniors:
"Do not even think about it!"
Yet welcome to the young:
"Take a seat and have a chat!"

Came a lad and said to the maiden:
"I am afraid you might be seeing someone

---

① Bipeng refers to the low stool made of split bamboo by the Dai.

怕你有了相好的吧?
他见了会打我!"

小姑娘拨了拨火,
低下头来对小伙子说:
"我倒是孤单单的一个,
就怕你有了老婆!"

"既然彼此都没有对象,
就应该诉一诉衷肠。"
他们就这样谈得知心,
一直谈到夜深……

第二天他拉着胡琴来了,
还是小伙子独自一人;
小姑娘一眼就认出了他,
而且懂得了他的真情。

"你若真心将我追求,
就该到我家竹楼,
去对我爹妈说说,
您是怎样爱我!"

"这时已经夜深人静,

古老的傣歌
Old Folk Songs of the Dai

Who would hit me in the face if seeing me here.

How dare I stay here for long!"

Poking the fire a little bit,

The maiden said with her head lowering down:

"All this time I have been single and alone.

I am afraid you might have tied the knot!"

"Now that both single are we,

Why not pour out each other's inner feelings?"

So, like bosom friends they talked,

Until midnight came…

Playing the wonderful music of the huqin,

Came the lad, alone, next day;

The girl recognized him at first sight,

And understood his feelings at once.

"If you truly do want to pursue me,

Then come to my house,

And tell my parents

How much you love me!"

"I would better not disturb your parents

不便打扰你的双亲；
我愿珍惜这样的时刻，
陪着你，看着你，直到天明……"

第三夜他带来了一管笛子，
站在竹箩边上发痴；
小姑娘猜到是有了喜事，
反而有点不好意思。

"我们两家长辈都合得来，
　如今就等媒人安排……"
小姑娘把她引进竹门，
火塘边又开始了细语低声①……

---

① 这是"婚歌"中的一个片段，下面是叙述说媒、结婚的过程。

古老的傣歌
Old Folk Songs of the Dai

At this moment when the evening grows late;

I would rather cherish the moment with you,

Until daybreak parts us…"

The boy brought a flute the third day,

Standing not far away, daydreaming;

Sensing that something she expected might come,

The fair maiden got a rosy color on her face.

"Now that both families get along well,

What we need is just a matchmaker…"

The girl invited him to the house,

And they whispered by the fire pit[①]…

[①] This is one scene of the Wedding Song. The following part depicts the process of the matchmaking and the wedding ceremony.

古歌 // Old Folk Songs of the Dai & the Naxi

一朵菊花 ①

男：
你可记得有人在南山等你？
砍柴时我们相逢在山上？

哦，北庄的姑娘，
你像金色的菊花一样漂亮；

你站在竹篱边，
像金菊秋天怒放；

---

① 此歌是流传在滇西德宏傣族自治区的一支古老的民歌。原名为"莫平仑"或"机侍达"，前者应译为"黄色的菊花"，后者应译为"开在眼前的一朵菊花"。这个歌，有的是一个人唱，以第三者的身份叙述这个故事；有的是男女对唱；有的在男女对唱中加上第三者的旁白。每种唱法和每个人唱的差别都很大，这里是根据刀秀庭、方福和、方爱德所唱整理的。

古老的傣歌
Old Folk Songs of the Dai

Song of a Chrysanthemum[①]

Male:

Do you remember me from South Mountain

Where we met and where I am still waiting for you?

O my fair maiden from the North Village,

As lovely as a golden chrysanthemum;

Standing beside the bamboo fence,

You shine like a golden chrysanthemum in full bloom;

---

① This is an ancient folk song popular in Dehong Dai Autonomous Region of west Yunnan Province. The song was originally named Mopinglun which means yellow chrysanthemum, or Jidaida which means the chrysanthemum at the moment of full bloom. The song could be sung by one singer as the third person narrating the story, or as the duet between a male and a female, sometimes an aside of the third person can also be added into the duet. Each way of singing as well as the unique style of each singer differs greatly. The song here was compiled based on the singing of Dao Xiuting, Fang Fuhe, and Fang Aide.

你披上披巾①，
像孔雀开屏一样；

别的花已经凋谢，
你却含苞欲放；

你是池中的莲花，
永远散着清香；

金耳鸟②在蓝天说话，
金菊花，是你对我歌唱！

金菊花，金菊花，
银马需要配上金鞍；

金菊花，你是匹银马，
可曾配到一副好鞍？

你若还没有，
快把你的项环拨响！

---

① 滇西的傣族妇女，有很多在肩上披上一块披巾作为装饰品。披巾有单色的，也有各种花色的；但有一种花丝绒的，颜色极像孔雀毛，很美。
② 傣话，一种会唱歌的鸟。黑毛、两耳各垂一片黄肉，又叫料哥。

古老的傣歌
Old Folk Songs of the Dai

Wearing a decorated shawl around the shoulder①,
You are a proud peacock showing your beautiful tail;

Even if all flowers fade away, you are
Always a flower bud ready to bloom;

You are as lovely as the lotus,
Tingeing the air with its delicate fragrance;

You are as lovely as the Golden Ear②,
Singing to me pleasantly in the sky!

My dear golden chrysanthemum,
Silver horse yearns for a golden saddle;

Like a silver horse you are to me,
A nice saddle have you found?

If not, my fair maiden, please
Ring your harness bell immediately!

---

① Most Dai women from west Yunnan Province like to wear shawls around shoulders for decoration. Some are monochromatic while others flowery. There is also a beautiful velvet-like one with the color resembling the feathers of peacock.
② It's the Dai language referring to a singing bird which has black feathers and a piece of yellow flesh hanging down its each ear. It is also called Liaoge.

古歌 // Old Folk Songs of the Dai & the Naxi

女：
自从那天相逢山上，
以后，再也无法将你遗忘。

我天天上那山砍柴，
那山的柴已被我砍光。

人家问我为什么还上那山，
哎，谁又知道我在怎么想……

你看到的这匹马哟，
当然要配一副好鞍，

但看过许多金鞍和银鞍，
可是没有一个适当！

男：
哦，我听见你的项环拨响，
我，已为你备下了好鞍——

金菊花，我就要到你跟前，
当月儿升在竹梢上。

古老的傣歌
Old Folk Songs of the Dai

Female:

Ever since we met on the hill the other day,

Impossible was it to get you out of my head.

Since then I collect firewood on that hill every day,

Until this day none can ever be found.

What I am driving at nobody knows,

Why I still go to that hill they just wonder…

The horse standing right in front of you

Surely deserves a good saddle,

Yet whatever golden and silver saddle I have seen before,

None of them were my perfect match!

Male:

Your bell ringing I surely did hear,

And already prepared you a perfect saddle.

When the moon rises above the bamboo,

I cannot wait to meet you, my golden chrysanthemum.

古歌 // Old Folk Songs of the Dai & the Naxi

我不挎刀，也不带枪①，
你听见玎②响，就是我到你门旁。

我是村里的歌手
献给你的是不停的歌唱。

我恨不得和鸟一样有翅膀，
能飞到你的身旁。

我唱了又吹，吹了有唱。
也不知道累，也不想歇。

哦，我那时什么都不知道，
周围的世界都已遗忘——

露水洒在花上，草上铺满寒霜，
半夜的狗，对我吠个不停，

饿着肚子，还不知饥寒，
只知道以后天已经大亮……

---

① 在老傣文中"枪"与"象脚鼓"同音、同字、不同义，所以也有译作象脚鼓的。
② 象脚鼓和玎都是傣族的乐器，后者极像三弦琴，声音优美。

古老的傣歌
Old Folk Songs of the Dai

Without carrying a dao or a qiang[①], I will
Show up at your door with the sound of the ding[②] playing.

As the singer living in the village,
My non-stop singing to you is all I can present.

I wish I could, like a bird,
Fly to your side, my dear.

I keep singing and playing
Without knowing exhaustion.

O the whole world I have utterly forgotten,
Let alone what happened around me then.

Dazzling dewdrops on the flowers, grass carpeted with frost,
And the dog barking outside all night long were out of my concern.

Eating nothing yet feeling no hunger or cold,
I came only to know that daybreak had come…

---

① In the ancient Dai language, "qiang" has the same pronunciation and character with the elephant-foot drum but differs in meaning. So, it is also translated as the elephant-foot drum.
② The elephant-foot drum and the ding are both musical instruments of the Dai. The latter has a beautiful sound resembling the sanxian, a three-stringed fretless plucked musical instrument.

古歌 // Old Folk Songs of the Dai & the Naxi

女：
哦，小伙子，你是在撒谎，
夜夜我等你都无法等上。

是你没找到我家的门？
还是你去串别家的姑娘？

我夜里等了又等，
等你的玎声飘来。

我等待乌云抱住月亮，
别让月亮看清出去串的姑娘①。

我卷着身子，等待你的披毯把我裹紧，
好把我带到另一个快乐的地方……

男：
哦，云雾已遮住那情侣对对双双，
只有我孤独地坐在山坡上。

金菊花，我多么想你，

---

① 傣族叫恋爱为"串姑娘"。通常在夜里，男的把女的约出家，男的用披毯把女的裹着，搂着出去。

古老的傣歌
Old Folk Songs of the Dai

Female:

Lad, no truth you are telling me,

Each night I wait for you but in vain.

Were you going to the wrong house

Or just pursuing other girls?

Until midnight I have waited and waited,

Looking forward to the familiar sound of the ding.

When dark clouds appeared in the sky,

Hiding those girls in romantic dates① from the moon.

I cuddled myself up, waiting for you to wrap me up

With your blanket on the way to our dreamland…

Male:

Clouds had hidden those couples from the moon,

Yet it was only me sitting alone on the hillside.

How much I miss you! Golden chrysanthemum,

---

① The Dai call dating as hanging out with girls (chuanguniang). They usually ask girls out in the midnight, wrapping them up in blankets and going out together.

想得我的肝肠也断。
如今，风在漫山地吹，
它能不能将我的歌送到你耳旁？

我想你，想到月亮落下山冈，
我想你，怨歌已唱疼了我的心房。

泼水节① 那天我到你家门前，
却瞭不见你的身影出现在竹楼上。

想泼水，找不到人泼，
我的怨气泼在你家竹篱上！

打着象脚鼓在你家门前转，
转了三圈啊，又走了三趟，

我面前走过一对又一双，
只有我孤零零地在你家门前彷徨……

女：
一年十二个月，一个月三十天，
你想我，可以随你想！

---

① 泼水节：在傣历新年中，男女互相泼水，人们找自己喜欢的人泼，泼得越湿越好。

古老的傣歌
Old Folk Songs of the Dai

No one knows what I painfully endure.
I wonder if the wind blowing over the mountain
Can carry my song to you, fair maiden.

The moon went down the hill, yet I still lay awake missing you,
Sad songs sung thousand times still couldn't make up for my missing you.

On the day of the Water-splashing Festival[①], I showed up at your door,
Yet found no trace of you upstairs by the window.

I splashed water on your bamboo fence
After finding nowhere to vent my anger!

Playing in despair the elephant-foot drum,
I kept pacing up and down by your house.

Seeing sweet couples walking by,
I had to wander at your door, alone with myself…

Female:

A year consists of twelve months, and a month thirty days,
On any of these days you can think of me!

---

① Water-splashing Festival: it is New Year's Day in the lunar calendar of the Dai. On that day, people splash water each other, particularly someone he or she has a crush on. It is said that the wetter you get, the luckier you will be.

我爱你，答应嫁给你，
父母却爱媒人的舌头长，

要抬来银子三千筐，
要抬来金子三千筐；

不然，他们不准我跟你，
说那是大象吃凤凰。

男：
哦，我哪来那么多金和银？
我却是一个好下力种地的男子汉！

我为你已盖好新竹楼，
我为你已开荒、插秧；

我等你来我家的那一天，
一同在竹林玩，学一对鸳鸯；

一边下力一边唱，
早晚不离你的身旁！

古老的傣歌
Old Folk Songs of the Dai

Yes will be my answer if you propose, brother dear,
Yet my parents favor the tittle-tattle of the matchmaker.

Only with three thousand baskets of silver,
As well as the same amount of solid gold;

Our marriage would then be blessed,
Otherwise sheer daydreaming it would be.

Male:
Silver and gold, I have none,
Yet I can stand on my own feet as a man!

A new home, built for us, has been completed,
And rocky land has been cleared for crops;

I expect you to come and spend time together at my house,
Or in the bamboo grove, as sweet a couple as mandarin ducks;

I will sing to you while farming,
By that time nothing can separate us!

女：
我也会为你舂白米，
我也会为你养个大金鸡；

我会帮你浇旱田，
把深谷的泉水引到旱地上；

不是我贪图银两，
可是没钱，爹妈要把我嫁到另一个村庄——

哦，雁群排着人字形来还让它那样回去，
别留下一只飞不回南方！

男：
怎么办呀，怎么办呀？
我没有钱啊！姑娘！

女：
为了我呀，为了我啊，
你就不能把别的办法想？

男：
哦，我还有一把钱，
可以放在你家饭甑和米臼里，

Female:

Let me do the pounding,

Let me raise chickens;

Let me divert the water from the valley,

Helping you water the dry land;

A money-worshiper I am not, yet without money,

I have to marry someone else but you!

Alas! I wish all the wild geese would fly back,

Never leaving one stay lonely in the north!

Male:

What should I do? What should I do?

Fair maiden, what should I do without money?

Female:

Could you figure out some ways

Just for my sake? Brother dear.

Male:

Well, I still have some savings left,

Let me hide them in the steamer and the mortar.

臼口好好遮住，
饭甑仍然放在铁锅上。
待明日你父母一看到这①，
就知道你已私奔到我家乡。

女：
可是父母知道了会追赶，
我俩是个怎样的下场？

为了以后不痛苦，
哥哥，别那样！

男：
父母追赶是我们的风俗，
虚赶，只是说你家的力量也强！

别担心，别害怕，
有什么事，我来抵挡！

女：
走！走！走！

---

① 傣族有偷婚的风俗，当父母看到这些标记，就知道女儿已随人逃跑。

Old Folk Songs of the Dai

Cover the mortar well, and

Keep still the steamer under the pan.

Then your parents will come to know everything

Once they notice the money hidden away[①].

Female:

I fear what we would end up with

If they run after us later?

To avoid agony endured later in life,

Please do not play stupid, my brother dear!

Male:

Parents chasing after us is the tradition,

And also the symbol of the family strength!

Do not be afraid, do not be worried,

You are not alone when facing all these troubles!

Female:

Alas! Where can we, I wonder,

---

① The Dai has the tradition of stealing marriage. When parents see these signs, they know that their daughter has eloped with someone.

我们要走到什么地方？

男：
看，前面走着我，后面跟着你，
像天上飞着鸟儿一双。

南山好采茶、插秧，
南山好盖屋、开荒；

我俩在南山上相识，
建立家，还在南山上。

……

Escape from the cruelty of reality?

Male:

I will lead you, and you follow me,

Just like lovely bird couples in the sky.

Let us settle on South Mountain

Where destiny allowed us to meet;

And where we can start afresh,

No need to fret how we will survive.

...

怨　歌

我们本来相亲相爱，
别人硬将我们拆开；
我喜欢你，你却离开了我，
妹啊，我是多么难过！

我像酒醉不醒，
我像得了疯病；
在家里，我待不住，
想出外，立不稳。

当我想起你，
我的心就发疼；
我俩希望成双，
偏偏折磨重重……

妹啊，香蕉已经熟透，
却被乌鸦啄烂；
前生注定的姻缘，

古老的傣歌
Old Folk Songs of the Dai

Sad Song about Love

We, supposed to love each other,
Were separated due to the third person;
I am in love with you who yet ended up leaving me,
How sorrowful I am right now! Sister dear!

Sometimes I lost myself like a drunken lunatic,
Sometimes I acted like a madman;
I could not stay at home for long,
Nor did I go out by myself.

My heart aches, sister dear,
When thinking of you;
A sweet couple as we would have been,
Yet end up enduring the agony of separation…

Bananas ripe and tempting on the tree
Were reduced to being destroyed by the crow;
Like us, fated to be together in another life,

却被坏人拆散!

妹啊,你怎能忍心离开?
妹啊,我要你打伙同在!
唉,别人都有幸福,
唉,而我只有悲哀!

妹啊,知了到时候都会叫,
你为什么到时候不理人了?
现在又是知了叫的时候,
你却把我丢在后脑!

我想你想得难受,
就像光着肩膀扛木料,
伤痕浸在汗水里,
浑身痛得发抖!

心爱的人儿被强占,
我落得一无所有、孤孤单单;
如今别人用藤圈把你套紧,
我想救你也近不了身!

我什么都不怕,
不怕毒蛇,不怕荨麻;

古老的傣歌
Old Folk Songs of the Dai

Yet still separated in this one!

How could you, my love, leave me so easily?
I wish to stay with you no matter what difficulties!
Alas! Everyone lives happily with their beloveds,
Yet only I live with solitary melancholy! Alas!

Cicadas sing while time matures,
Yet why did you ignore me all of a sudden?
Now it is the time of cicada singing again,
Yet I still have not heard from you!

What I am suffering right now you have no idea,
I am trembling in pain missing you,
Like pain from sweat touching the wounds
From carrying wood on bare shoulders!

Separated from you, my beloved,
I end up having nothing but loneliness;
I could not get you free either, since
Someone has kept a close eye on you.

Neither serpent nor poisonous nettle,
Nothing should I be afraid of;

就怕你变了心,
就怕你不理人!

可惜啊,太可惜!
金子中了毒变成了黑色!
可惜啊,太可惜!
成块的金子被研成粉屑!

妹啊,我爱你的黑眼睛,
你为什么丢掉你爱过的人?
妹啊,你的臂膀多么白嫩,
如今却被人加上锁链!

妹啊,烧山的野火太无情!
为什么把好柴也烧成灰烬?
可惜啊,太可惜!你失去了自由,
也失去了真正爱你的人!

妹啊,你把生长你的寨子抛弃了!
你把宽广的坪地抛弃了!
你把呜呜叫的纺车抛弃了!
你把来串门的小伙子抛弃了!

妹啊,你的头原来很好看,

古老的傣歌
Old Folk Songs of the Dai

Except you letting go of our promise,

And erasing me from your mind!

Shame! What a shame!

Gold turns black once exposed to poison!

Shame! What a shame!

A whole piece of gold has been ground to powder!

Sister dear, I am deeply attracted to your black eyes.

Why did you give up your beloved one?

Sister dear, such a white and tender shoulder you have,

But it has been fettered by someone you love not!

Sister dear, how ruthless the wild fire is,

Even turning the best wood into ashes!

What a shame! It is freedom that you have lost,

And someone you should spend the rest of your life with!

Sister dear, you leave the village you grew up in!

You forget the square where you often played on!

You leave behind your cherished spinning wheel!

And you abandon the lad once you loved!

How much I loved, sister dear,

可是你糟踏了自己的花冠；
你的头发现在好乱哟，
简直像个鸟雀窝！

妹啊，你要丢就丢到底！
把岩坡、山地都丢掉！
把那石滩上的流水也丢掉！
把那驮你走的好马也丢掉！

妹啊！你把这些丢干净，
再丢掉你嫁的那个男人！
我爱你的心永远不变，
妹啊，快回到我的身边！

唉，哥哥可怜的妹子哟，
你也可怜我这单身汉吧；
我在森林和四处流浪，
日夜把你思想……

你就像一颗明亮的珍珠，
丢在河中，被青苔裹住；
我想找你又没有办法，
汹涌的河水断了去路！

古老的傣歌
Old Folk Songs of the Dai

Your nice fair hair before,

Yet now it looks so bad like a bird's nest

Only by your heartlessly ruining the tiara on your head!

I dare you, sister dear, to abandon the whole world!

Either the hillside or the mountain,

Or the stream running over the rock,

Or the dear horse you have been riding!

I hope, sister dear, that you will abandon them all,

Including the man you married!

My love to you endures no matter what,

Come back, sister dear, into my arms!

Alas! So please, my poor sister,

Have some mercy on the single man

Who wanders aimlessly around,

Thinking of you night after night…

A brilliant pearl once you must have been,

Yet thrown away in the river and entangled by moss;

The turbulent flow blocks my way forward,

Making slim the chance of looking for you!

如果你有心把我爱，
你就该顺水淌下来，
我会和波浪搏斗，
把你紧紧抱在胸怀！

那时，我会变作一只小船，
我会把你驮上岸来；
假若一切都不是这样，
我就不算个男子汉！

我和你像树胶粘黏，
可是你和你丈夫藕断丝连；
为什么不把你丈夫丢下？
难道你怕他把我杀啦？

要是我死了，我就变成蚂蚁；
爬上树梢去等你，
等你坐到树荫下，
我就掉下来和你坐一起。

要是你丈夫把蚂蚁踩死，
那我就变成小蛇一条；
躲在草垫下面，
再把你来纠缠。

古老的傣歌
Old Folk Songs of the Dai

If you, my girl, love me back,
You should flow downstream.
And I will do what it takes to fight with the waves,
Only to hold you tightly in my arms!

I would rather become a boat then,
Carrying you ashore safely;
If I fail to keep my promise,
How can I stand as a man in the world?

I used to stay with you, never separating,
Yet now you are living with your husband;
Why not leave him behind instead, sister dear?
Are you afraid of him taking revenge on me?

I would become an ant if I died one day,
Waiting for you on the tree.
When you take a rest in the shade,
I will fall down and sit with you.

If your ruthless husband stomped on me,
A little snake I would turn into,
Hiding under the straw mattress,
And ruining the life you and your husband live.

古歌 // Old Folk Songs of the Dai & the Naxi

要是你丈夫还要行凶，
那我就化作一条蛟龙；
等待你来挑水或是洗衣，
卷一个浪头把你带去！

要不，我就要去打仗，
把我自己变成碉堡；
在进攻中直到刀刃砍断，
只剩下镂花的刀鞘！

假若我真的被人击中，
我的血也要把江水染红；
请你把我装进棺木里，
莫让乌鸦来啄食我的尸体！

假若竟然是你先死去，
我一定把你抱进攀枝花堆；
待一阵清风吹来，
将你和茸毛一道送上天际。

但愿你在天上也等着我，
我将立刻把你追随。

古老的傣歌
Old Folk Songs of the Dai

If your cruel husband still chased after me,

A Jiaolong① I would turn into;

Waiting for you to carry water or to do laundry,

And sweeping you along in the river!

Or I will let myself go to war,

Turning into a blockhouse defending against enemies;

Until my blade cut off in the attack,

I will leave nothing but an ornamentally-engraved scabbard!

If I were attacked by the enemy,

Dyeing the river red with my blood;

Please, my dear, keep my body in a coffin,

Away from the raven's pecking!

If you, sister dear, left the world before me,

I would bury you in cotton silk;

When comes the gentle and fresh breeze, it will

Bring you along with the cotton flowers to heaven.

Please wait for me out there, my love,

I will follow your step right after.

---

① A legendary river dragon in Chinese mythology. –Translator's note

唉，唉，可是你已经有了丈夫，
这一切都是枉费心机。

……

古老的傣歌
Old Folk Songs of the Dai

Yet, alas, someone other than me you have married,
What I have planned is nothing but sheer daydreaming.

…

古歌 // Old Folk Songs of the Dai & the Naxi

传　歌

我们从内地来，
我们有一万户；
我们从汉人地区来，
我们这里叫景洪。

据说我们祖先是皇帝，
皇儿以射弩将土地分封；
谁的弩箭落在哪里，
哪里就属他们弟兄。

长子的箭落在内地，
二儿子的箭落在另一块疆土，
幺儿射出最后一箭，
他的箭啊就落在帕罕①。

于是他带领四万五千人，
来寻找这一支弩箭；

---

① 帕罕：据说是现在的宣慰街，距车里十五华里。

古老的傣歌
Old Folk Songs of the Dai

Song of a Legend

Coming from the inland
Where Han people reside;
We now live in Jinghong,
Where people of 10 thousand dwell.

Our ancestor, it is said, was an emperor,
Who distributed land to his sons according to their archery skills;
The spot where the arrow finally dropped
Was where his son finally settled down.

The arrow shot by the eldest dropped inland,
And his younger brother in the realm of another territory,
Whereas the youngest shot the last arrow,
Which dropped in Pahan[①] which we know as Jinghong today.

Bringing 45 thousand people along with him,
The youngest was looking for his arrow;

---

① Pahan: it is now known as Xuanwei Street, 7.5 kilometers away from Cheli.

古歌 // Old Folk Songs of the Dai & the Naxi

从此他和这四万五千人，
在景洪，子孙繁衍①。
……

---

① 这首歌仅仅是西双版纳傣族历史传说中的一个片段。

古老的傣歌
Old Folk Songs of the Dai

He, along with his people, settled down there

Where generations of descendants have grown up since then[1].

…

---

[1] The song is only one extract from historic legends of the Dai in Xishuangbanna.

古歌 // Old Folk Songs of the Dai & the Naxi

战　歌

……
年代不必提及，
姓名不要详报①，
有两兄弟为夺取官位而抢杀，
战火就在这里燃烧！

荣誉啊！虚假的荣誉啊！
教兄弟都当作仇人了；
他们互相烧杀，互相不饶，
在战争中，人命旦夕难保！

母亲送儿子出征，
妻子送丈夫出门，
去了男人，竹楼是那么空寂，
可是又来抢杀的男人！

火，烧着这里的竹楼，

---

① 这是传歌中描写一百多年前一段混战中的一个片段。

古老的傣歌
Old Folk Songs of the Dai

Song of War

...

Mention not the year,

Nor dwell on the names of people[①],

It started as two brothers fought for honors,

And here gunfire and looting just happened!

Turning brothers against each other

Just for honor! What a meaningless act!

They mercilessly killed each other,

Causing more death of innocent people in the war!

Mothers shed tears for sons leaving for battle,

And wives hated to part with their beloveds,

Leaving their sweet homes in deadly quietude,

And occupied by looters from another village!

Looters set fire on houses of the locals,

---

① It is extracted from *Song of a Legend* depicting the war over a century ago.

刀，砍向人们的胸膛，
年轻的女人受不了污辱，
奋身投入澜沧江……

澜沧江，你日夜流，
流不完我们的眼泪和悲伤；
澜沧江，你不再流那黄色的水，
而是你子女的血浆！

澜沧江，来杀人的男人，
也是你养育大的；
女人啊，当你儿媳投江，
你可想到你儿子在烧杀别人的村庄？

他持火烧着了别人的草房，
他的刀正对着别人的胸膛，
在那里，也有人受了他的污辱
去投江，像他的女人一样……

女人啊，你做了错事一桩，
强盗的战争把你儿子变成强盗一样；
母亲等儿子再也等不回来，
只有仇恨记在她心上！

And waved their swords at innocent people.

Young women, bearing no more humiliation,

Jumped into the Lancang River without a second thought…

Lancang River, you never stopped flowing,

Yet still could not equal our tears shed;

Lancang River, what flowed in you was not yellow water,

But the blood of your descendants!

Men who came here slaughtering,

Were fed by you too, Mother River;

Poor women, when your daughter-in-law gave up her life,

Did it occur to you that your son was burning and slaughtering too?

He burned people's houses, leaving them homeless,

He waved the sword at the innocents, taking their lives.

Poor women there, like his wife back at home,

Could not bear the humiliation and jumped in the river…

What a huge mistake you had made! Poor women!

A ruthless looter the war has turned your son into;

Once so slim the chance of awaiting his son's return,

The poor mother held nothing but grudges in her heart!

可是，你再教儿孙报仇，
只能报那些带给我们战争的人的仇，
不然，官方的战争成了我们的战争，
互相烧、杀，怎么受得了！

……

古老的傣歌
Old Folk Songs of the Dai

If you, however, counted on your offspring to take revenge,

Please target just those who brought us war,

Most victims, otherwise, would be innocent civilians

Who stood no more burning and killing each other in the war!

...

古歌 // Old Folk Songs of the Dai & the Naxi

盖 屋

刮风下雨的夜晚,
家家都已安眠;
独有这家的两口子,
还在枕边低声盘算。

别人都盖了新屋子,
为什么我们住破屋?
又不是我们没有双手!
劳动不如别人!

应该盖幢新屋子,
应该盖幢好屋子;
结结实实的屋子,
明明亮亮的屋子。

盼到三月间,
拣个街子天,
找着生意人,

古老的傣歌
Old Folk Songs of the Dai

House Building Song

Every household was falling into deep sleep
On a windy and rainy night;
Only one couple still stayed wide awake,
Whispering to each other something important.

New houses our neighbors have built and lived in,
Yet why do we still live in a shabby one?
We do have our own hands!
We can work on our own like others do!

We should build a new house,
A house better than we used to live in;
A house stronger than we used to live in,
And a house brighter than we used to live in.

When March arrives,
Let us go on a market day,
To buy some cast iron

生铁买几斤。

买铁干什么?
买铁打砍刀。
打刀干什么?
打刀砍木料。

生铁放在炉子里炼,
砍刀磨得明闪闪。
砍竹子要赶三月间,
割茅草莫误了四月天。

细心割下茅草,
一根一根理好;
回家编成草排,
一排一排码高。

丈夫走山路哟,
为的是砍伐木料;
老婆整天火塘边忙哟,
为的是预备干粮。

一袋子糯米,
一袋子辣椒,

古老的傣歌
Old Folk Songs of the Dai

From the dealer appropriate.

What is the cast iron for?
It is for forging a machete.
And what is the machete for?
It is for cutting wood.

In the stove, iron was being refined,
Machete, sharpened enough, was prepared.
Bamboo should be cut in March,
And straw mowed in April.

Straw cut and piled,
Was put in good shape;
One layer after another,
Was piled high and neat.

My darling, for collecting enough wood,
You risked walking mountain roads;
I, in order to prepare more food,
Kept busy in the kitchen all day long.

A bag of sticky rice,
A bag of chilies.

盐巴、猪油、咸菜不能少,
芝麻、酸笋、芭蕉也带了。

第二天的早晨,
背起袋子启程,
走进了老林,
先搭个窝棚安身。

把麻栗树都砍倒,
在地上再选过一道;
要直的、白的、结实的,
做椽子才牢靠。

先要有个好爸爸,
尔后才有好儿子;
先要有些好料子,
尔后才有好房子。

料子已经备齐,
立刻回到寨里。
人多力气大,
大家相帮抬一下吧。

听说盖新屋,

古老的傣歌
Old Folk Songs of the Dai

Do not forget salt, lard, pickles,

As well as sesame, sour bamboo shoots and bananas.

Arriving in the morning of the following day,

He took off, with his belongings.

After entering the woods,

A shed he built and settled down first.

Cutting some teak trees down,

And out of which selected the best;

Something straight, white, and strong

Was the perfect material for the rafters.

A sensible good child is surely

Brought up by understanding parents;

Likewise, strong and nice houses

Are built out of prized materials.

Having selected and prepared for the wood needed,

The master of the house returned right away.

Neighbors heard and came from all directions,

Helping him carry building materials.

Once a new house was being built,

人人来帮助；
白头发，黑头发，
老的少的都参加。

小姑娘打扮漂亮，
小伙子穿着倜傥，
拉木料是个好机会啊，
谈情说爱多欢畅！

木料抬进寨子里边，
白花花一片真是晃眼；
墨斗纵横拉线，
锯子来回解板。

大小尺寸都合意，
就等动手下脚基；
浑身干净、换套新衣，
请博赞[①]卜卦去。

博赞数了数米[②]，
决定了吉利时日，
牛角一吹嘟嘟响，

[①] 博赞，是西双版纳傣族农村中的巫师。
[②] 博赞卜卦时，主要是看米的数目，逢双则主吉兆。

古老的傣歌
Old Folk Songs of the Dai

Everyone came to give a hand;

Both the young and the old

Came to do a good turn.

Young girls dressed up elaborately,

While boys looked shining in their attire,

During the course of carrying wood,

They grasped the chance to know each other!

Wood carried to the village,

Glistening under the sun;

Clear and bold marks were made by the ink marker,

While hacksaw was ready to split wood up.

While wood of each size was prepared,

We were ready to build a concrete foundation;

Taking a bath and changing into new clothes beforehand,

We were heading to invite Bozan[1] for divination.

Counting the grains of rice[2],

Bozan chose the date deemed to be a lucky day.

Hearing the horn blown,

---

[1] Bozan is the wizard in Dai villages in Xishuangbanna.
[2] It's mainly the number of rice that Bozan depends on when seeking divination. Even number forebodes auspiciousness.

古歌 // Old Folk Songs of the Dai & the Naxi

召来了全寨男女。

小伙子挖土下脚基，
小姑娘挑水来和泥；
小娃娃摘来芭蕉叶，
为的是中午的立柱礼。①

立了柱子上椽子，
上了椽子搭架子。
屋脊梁上安杈子，
来年好歇小燕子。

钉了桁条上草排，
草排不偏也不歪；
一层一层要分明，
就像梭罗布②的花纹。

多谢乡亲和诸友，
唯愿新屋住长久；
爬下屋顶洗洗手，
坐下先敬一壶酒。

① 傣人盖新屋时，立柱的仪式很隆重，要以芭蕉叶裹着柱子，祈望新居清吉。
② 梭罗布是傣族妇女用木机织的一种土布。

古老的傣歌
Old Folk Songs of the Dai

Everyone from the village gathered around.

Young boys started to lay a foundation,
Girls carried water to mix clay;
And little children brought banana leaves picked
For the ceremony of column erection[①] at noon.

Column erection was followed by rafter landing,
Then the framework was constructed right after.
Then some branches were put on the ridge
For the sweet home of swallows in the coming year.

Beams nailed before neatly organized straw
Was placed on the roof of the house;
The roof was covered with straw, layer by layer,
Like the decorated patterns of Suoluo cloth[②].

Great thanks were granted to neighbors and friends,
Wishing a sturdy house built to live in;
The master washed his hands after climbing down the roof,
And made a toast to all coming to help.

---

① The ceremony of column erection, when the Dai were building a new house, is magnificent. Usually they wrap the column with banana leaves, praying for peace and auspiciousness of the family.
② Suoluo cloth is the traditional cloth Dai women weave with the wooden loom.

古歌 // Old Folk Songs of the Dai & the Naxi

这个说主人家粮食满囤，
那个说主人家牛马成群；
万种瘟病都不沾身，
灾难祸患全给我滚！

门外竖起竹篾笆，
屋里搭起三脚架；
三块石头三只脚，
一只脚要说一句吉利话。

头一只脚是赤金，
二一只脚是纹银，
三一只脚是宝石，
三只脚都带来好光景！

古老的傣歌
Old Folk Songs of the Dai

People gave their best wishes,

Wishing the master abundant food and livestock;

Wishing the master good health forever,

As well as no disasters and troubles!

Outside the house was built the bamboo fence,

While inside the home stood a three-legged stool;

Each leg, it was said, of the stool

Indicates something auspicious about the household.

All three legs would foresee a bright future!

The first one stood for gold,

The second for silver,

And the last for gemstones.

纳西古歌三首
Three Old Folk Songs of the Naxi

古歌 // Old Folk Songs of the Dai & the Naxi

达勒·乌萨米

一

天上有七个星星,
妈妈养下七个姑娘。

七个星星比不上一个月亮,
七姊妹要数老大强——

大姐叫乌萨米,
白得像玉龙山上的雪一样;

大姐乌萨米,
牙齿长得像一颗颗糯米一样;

大姐乌萨米,
她一笑,花也开了;

大姐乌萨米,
眼睛像镜子一样明亮;

纳西古歌三首
Three Old Folk Songs of the Naxi

Wusami of Dale

I

Under one roof there once lived seven sisters,
Just like seven stars twinkling in the sky.

Seven stars were not as bright as the moon,
Likewise, the eldest was the backbone of the family.

Known as Wusami, the eldest sister
Was as fair as the snow on Yulong Mountain;

Wusami, the eldest sister
Had teeth as white and neat as the sticky rice;

Wusami, the eldest sister
Smiled like a flower blossom;

Wusami, the eldest sister
Had eyes as bright as mirrors;

大姐乌萨米,
胆子大,像男人一样。

她一眨眼,就上了山一趟,
给家里捡回了柴一筐。

她仿佛还没有起床,
厨房的水就已经满了缸。

她播种,一播一大把,
她栽秧,一手栽十行。

她播的种,每颗种子都长得好,
她栽的秧,比别人栽的长得旺。

她绣的花,像真的一样,
绣的鸟会飞,绣的花也香。

爹妈没儿子,可有这么好的姑娘,
她是爹妈的囡,又是一家之长。

她是六个妹妹的姐姐,
又有母亲一样的心肠。

纳西古歌三首
Three Old Folk Songs of the Naxi

Wusami, the eldest sister
Had the nerve of men.

With just a moment's notice, dear Wusami
Had carried home a stack of firewood.

Still into sound sleep was everyone, yet
Wusami had filled up the water tank in the kitchen.

She sowed, all by herself,
She planted, neat and quick.

The seedlings Wusami sowed grew up well,
And what she planted grew fatter and taller.

As vivid as the real, flowers Wusami embroidered
Smelled good and birds seemed to fly.

No sons born though, parents viewed her as treasured possession,
Wusami was the dear daughter of her parents, and the eldest.

As the eldest of the family, Wusami
Gave motherly love to her six younger sisters.

除了不吃她的奶，
六个妹妹都靠她抚养。

屎一把，尿一把，
把六个妹妹养大。

人人都说乌萨米有八只手，
人人都说乌萨米有八只脚。

乌萨米，人人夸，
谁不夸她是最好的姑娘。

老年人都说她是自己的囡，
年轻人都说她是自己的姐姐。

乌萨米生在达勒地方，
人人都说她是达勒的女儿……

二

天上有乌云是要下雨，
雨后的晴天一定有长虹——

纳西古歌三首
Three Old Folk Songs of the Naxi

Except breast feeding, Wusami
Had raised her six little sisters.

Undergoing all sorts of hardships, Wusami
Had brought up her six little sisters.

Speaking highly of her, everyone said
She was as capable as having eight hands and eight feet.

Speaking highly of her, everyone said
She was the best girl they have ever met.

She was the dear daughter to the senior,
And the sweet sister to the youngster.

Born and brought up in Dale, Wusami
Was the daughter of her dear hometown…

II

From dark clouds people sense a rainy day,
And a sunny day after the rain anticipates a rainbow.

姑娘的脸上常常泛红晕，
姑娘的心啊，已经和孩子不同……

她见着男人总低着头，
身子还会扭扭动。

仿佛你一望她，
她便失去了三分美色；

仿佛你再看她，
她便怕落在你的手中。

六个妹妹整天在一起议论，
什么人才能做她们的姐夫。

狗在门口一吠，
就把六个妹妹惊动：

"是不是有人来说媒了？
姐姐，快把头梳一梳。"

早上喜鹊在枝头叫，
妹妹喜得嘴都合不拢：

纳西古歌三首
Three Old Folk Songs of the Naxi

Face turning red from shyness quite often, Wusami
Had blossomed into a young lady, not a child any more...

Always keeping her head low, Wusami
Turned coy and shy to look into the eyes of men.

It seemed her beauty faded while
People looked into her beautiful eyes;

It seemed she was afraid to get her heart stolen
If people could not take their eyes off her.

The other six sisters wondered all day long
Who would be the beloved of their dear sister.

Hearing the dog barking at the doorway,
The six sisters sat up and gossiped:

"Does anyone come matchmaking?
Sister Wusami, dress up please!"

Hearing the magpie singing in the morning on the tree,
So delighted were the six sisters:

"姐姐,一定是你合意的人,
来到我们家中!"

门口有马蹄声震动,
妹妹都挤在一起,眼睛贴着门缝:

"马上下来的人该是姐夫吧,
看样子,不是将军,也是英雄……"

她们常常围住姐姐,
给姐姐梳梳头发。

她们上山砍柴回来,
总给姐姐带回一朵山茶。

妹妹也问姐姐:
"你要选个什么样的姐夫?"

"我要选的人呀——"
她没说完话,脸就遮住:

"还没出嫁的姑娘说这话,
害羞呀!害羞!"

纳西古歌三首
Three Old Folk Songs of the Naxi

"Sister Wusami, there must be
Someone you adore coming!"

With the clip-clop of the horse coming near,
The six sisters gathered and peeked through the door:

"The man on the horse must be our brother-in-law,
Either a general or a hero he might be…"

Sitting around sister Wusami more often,
The six sisters liked to tidy her hair.

Each time when collecting firewood back home,
A camellia they would bring back for Wusami.

The six girls kept asking their sister:
"Who is going to be our brother-in-law?"

"I would like to choose someone…"
Stopped Wusami unexpectedly with her flushed face hidden:

"Still a maiden am I, too shy,
Too shy am I to say it aloud!"

哦,姑娘大了就要出嫁呀,
害羞,怕是假的吧!

哦,姑娘大了就要出嫁,
害羞,又有什么用!

媒人一天来三个,
媒人三天来九个。

再过三天姑娘长得更好看,
媒人一天来了九十九个。

九十九个媒人是九十九个男人的心,
九十九个男人把乌萨米的父母缠住。

九十九个男人都发誓——
一定要把她娶到手。

九十九个男人都说:
娶到乌萨米,一生都幸福。

可是乌萨米不能嫁给九十九个男人,
乌萨米只能选一个丈夫。

纳西古歌三首
Three Old Folk Songs of the Naxi

O there was no reason to feel shy,
Since girls growing up married anyway!

O it was meaningless to feel shy,
Since girls growing up married anyway!

Three matchmakers came one day,
And by the third day there came nine.

More and more attractive Wusami had become,
So the matchmakers added up to 99 per day.

99 matchmakers spoke for 99 men who
Ingratiated themselves with Wusami's parents.

Came and swore these 99 men that
They must marry no one but Wusami.

Came and said these 99 men that
An entire life would be happy to marry Wusami.

Wusami, however, could not marry 99 men,
Only one she could have at last.

九十九个男人没有一个她爱,
她爱的人,早已在她心中。

媒人刚上门就带来聘礼,
九十九双鞋,九十九件衣服。

乌萨米见聘礼就哭,
乌萨米见媒人就哭。

娘问囡:"你有什么事,
为什么这样痛苦?

"有这么多媒人上门,
是囡和爹妈的体面。

"九十九个男人由你挑,
你还不高兴?"

"我不愿嫁出门一步,
愿终身将二老服侍!

"等六个妹妹都找到好婆家,
我再出嫁也不迟!"

纳西古歌三首
Three Old Folk Songs of the Naxi

The truth is, the heart of Wusami had long

Belonged to someone other than these 99 men.

99 pairs of shoes, along with 99 sets of clothes,

Are the betrothal gifts matchmakers brought to Wusami.

Yet Wusami shed tears in despair,

Seeing matchmakers coming with gifts.

"Why are you feeling so sad?"

Asked the mother of Wusami.

"99 men came and proposed,

We should be proud of it!

"99 choices available for you,

Why are you not happy and satisfied?"

"I would rather spend my entire life

Taking care of you two, my dear parents.

"Or I will consider myself only

After my six sisters find their beloveds!"

"囡啊,你尽说些傻话,
错过了时机,你将来要怨恨父母!

"不能做衣服的布叫什么布?
不嫁男人的姑娘叫什么女人?

"在家,你是亲父母,
出了嫁,丈夫亲过父母;

"等你有了三男二女,
儿子又亲过丈夫!

"囡啊,你是姑娘该有女人的心呀,
再想想呀,别这么糊涂!"

囡听了,一刻哭了三次,
囡听了,一天哭了九场。

不是姑娘不长女人的心,
不是她是个不爱男人的姑娘。

只是九十九个当中没她心爱的,
她爱的人,早在她心上。

纳西古歌三首
Three Old Folk Songs of the Naxi

"Failing to grab the chance, my silly daughter,
You would blame us one day!

"Cloth is meant to make clothes, and
Girls growing up are supposed to wed one day.

"Parents, the closest back at home, are
Replaced by husband after marriage;

"Husband, ultimately, loses his position
After children come to the family!

"A woman's heart you should have, my silly daughter,
And think carefully before your decision!"

Her parents' words made Wusami weep three times in a quarter of
    an hour,
And nine times had she shed tears in a day.

Wusami had a woman's heart indeed,
And a heart for the man she did have too.

The one Wusami loved, yet not from the 99 men,
Had had long stolen her heart.

只是九十九个还差一个,
九十九个合起来也没有那个人强。

九十九个当中就是没有他,
他,牵着姑娘的肝肠。

姑娘不愿出嫁是假的,
只是心爱的人不在身旁。

姑娘不愿出嫁也是真的,
嫁她不爱的人,跟嫁给鬼一样。

要是爱她的人托媒人上门,
姑娘马上就不哭了;

要是爱她的人托媒人上门,
姑娘还没揩眼泪就笑了。

三

姑娘所爱的男人是谁,
她连名字也无法说上。

一天,姑娘在锄地,

纳西古歌三首
Three Old Folk Songs of the Naxi

　Among 99 men who came to propose,
None was comparable to the one she cared for.

Among 99 men who came to propose,
None was comparable to the one she concerned.

Not true was Wusami reluctant to marry,
Since the one she loved was nowhere to be found.

Yet true was Wusami reluctant to marry,
Since it meant a nightmare to marry someone she loved not.

If the matchmaker came to speak for her beloved,
Wusami would stop weeping right away;

If the matchmaker came to speak for her beloved,
Wusami would smile with tears still on her face.

III

The man Wusami had long had feelings for
Was someone whose name was yet unknown.

It all started one day when a man came by

古歌 // Old Folk Songs of the Dai & the Naxi

一个人走过她身旁。

姑娘一锄下去挖二尺深,
一个人顶上三个男子汉。

姑娘一锄下去挖二尺深,
禾苗跟着就在长。

路边的人赞扬了一声,
姑娘低着头不吭;

路边的人赞扬了两句,
姑娘瞥了这个男人一眼;

路边的人夸了三次,
姑娘"咯咯"地笑了九声。

青藤搭上了架子,
姑娘和这个男人已相识。

面团在一起结成疙瘩,
这两人就搭上了话:

"过路的人啊,

纳西古歌三首
Three Old Folk Songs of the Naxi

While she was busy hoeing.

With the strength of three men put together,
Wusami hoed the land two feet deep.

And Wusami hoed the land two feet deep,
Immediately the seedlings started to grow up.

Stopped and given a compliment by the man,
Wusami ignored and uttered no words;

Not until a further compliment was given
Did Wusami take a glance at him nearby;

She could not help giggling while
Being complimented thrice by the man.

It was the time when the vine crawled on the shelf
That Wusami was acquainted with her man of fate.

Like paste forms the moment when flour meets water,
The two of them chatted nonstop as they met:

"O where are you going, passer-by?

古歌 // Old Folk Songs of the Dai & the Naxi

你站在这里,是想找哪一家?

"你是迷了路摸不到方向,
还是歇凉,在我们槐荫下?"

"我不是迷了路摸不到方向,
我不是歇凉槐荫下。

我不来村里寻找哪一家,
只在等待夕阳西下!"

"你看太阳刚从东山升上,
等夕阳,得等到什么时光?

"你没事,为什么一直等着它,
难道只为了看那一瞬霞光!"

"晚霞虽美,已近黄昏,
看你却能看到明天天亮。

"姑娘,我走了,
明天相逢还在这个地方。"

第二天他来了片刻又要走,

纳西古歌三首
Three Old Folk Songs of the Naxi

Why are you standing here?

Are you lost or just taking a break
In the shade of the pagoda tree here?"

"I am not lost in the middle of nowhere,
Nor do I take a break in the shade of the pagoda tree.

I am here not for anyone in the village,
But waiting for the beautiful setting sun!"

"But the sun has just risen from the east,
Quite long, I am afraid, you have to wait!

What is worth keeping you waiting here?
A moment's twilight was not what I expected you to say!"

"The rosy sunset, though stunning, disappears at dusk,
Yet with you I can stay until daybreak comes.

I am leaving, dear maiden, yet
I promise to meet you here tomorrow."

The next day the man did come,

神色是那么忧伤。

姑娘问:"你为什么走得这么匆忙?
有什么事,使你不舒畅?"

"哎,前面有家人家孩子病了,
没钱看病,还缺柴缺粮。

"我得赶忙给他送些钱去,
帮助他们度过这难熬的时光!"

"这一次,难道我也留不下你,
好让你看看今天的夕阳!"

"正因为不说谎,我才到这里来,
正因为你,我特地拐过这个地方。

"要不是你,我已经到那家人家了;
要不是你,谁能把我牵回这个地方?"

四

这天回去,他晚上又来了,
孤独地踏着冷月。

纳西古歌三首
Three Old Folk Songs of the Naxi

Yet he left soon with a tinge of sadness on his face.

"Why are you in such a hurry to leave?
Did anything bad happen?" Asked the maiden.

"A poor child is ill, and what is worse, his family
Has no money to see a doctor and food is scarce.

I am about to give them some money soon,
Helping them get through the difficult time!"

"Even I could not keep you this time
To watch together the beautiful sunset!"

"I kept my word so I came here,
I came all the way just to see you.

I would, but for you, have arrived at their place.
Who else has the charm to attract me here but you?"

IV

The man, accompanied by the cold moon,
Returned that night all by himself.

古歌 // Old Folk Songs of the Dai & the Naxi

露水湿了田埂、篱笆,
露水冻了他的双手。

等待她回一句话,
却只见月光下田中的水花。

他叫了一声没有人答应,
他感到失去了她多孤独!

他今日孤独得多可怜,
一个人冷凄凄地扶住篱笆。

半生都在四处奔走,颠沛流离,
三十多年还没有个家!

说简单也十分简单,
一男一女并在一起就成啦!

可是年轻时奔走前途打光棍,
今天年纪又有了一大把!

如今走来这里寻自己的家门,
这里像没有谁认识他!

纳西古歌三首
Three Old Folk Songs of the Naxi

Drenching the ridge as well as the fence,
The dewdrops made his hands frozen with cold.

Expecting to get an answer from the maiden, he
Saw only water splashing in the field under the moonlight.

No response came after the man called. He dared not
Imagine how lonely it would be to lose her!

Leaning against the fence waiting with bitter coldness,
What a poor man he was today in lonely solitude!

Spending most of his lives drifting around,
So much had the man expected to settle in his thirties.

Easy, in fact, it would be to realize the wish,
As long as he found his other half in life.

The man yet spent too much time on his career,
Winding up a poor bachelor still in his thirties!

Now he came to look for his family clan,
Yet no one seemed to know him well!

哎，家里现在还不知道有什么事？
回去吧！回去吧？

以后，老是不见他来，
姑娘在田里空等待……

一等，姑娘不见他来，
再等，姑娘的心要碎：

"为什么？为什么啊？
为什么他不来看看我！"

每天刚出太阳，
姑娘就倚着锄头在田畔。

妹妹说："那块地上的活已做完了，
姐姐，你怎么老上那块地去？"

哦，姑娘和那个人在这里相识，
她想着，相逢也一定在这地方。

可是，等一天不见他来，
等了两天，姑娘急不可待。

纳西古歌三首
Three Old Folk Songs of the Naxi

Caring about his family members back at home,
The man made the hard choice to go back then.

Later came the maiden and waited in the field,
Waiting for the man who did not show up at all…

Seeing him not come to meet her,
Heartbroken was the maiden who kept waiting.

"Why? Alas! Why?
Why does he not come to see me?"

Each morning when the sun rose in the east,
Wusami leaned against the hoe waiting in the field.

"You have finished your work in that field,
Why do you still go there?" asked her sister.

Knowing him, the maiden thought, right here,
Destiny might allow them to meet here again.

The first day, however, the man came not,
And two days later the maiden became anxious.

姑娘真怕他把自己忘记,
姑娘真怕再等他也不来。

从黎明等到太阳落,
从黑夜等到东方白。

姑娘一刻哭了三次,
姑娘一天哭了九场。

姑娘想着他的模样,
年纪和他叔叔有些相仿。

可是只要看他一眼,
姑娘自己就年轻了几岁。

可是只要看看他的眼睛,
就知道他的年纪比胡子少得多。

可是只要看看他的眼睛,
就知道他爱上了姑娘一个……

纳西古歌三首
Three Old Folk Songs of the Naxi

She was afraid of being forgotten by the man,
She feared never seeing him again in her lifetime.

From dawn till dusk and from night till daybreak,
Wusami kept waiting and waiting all the time.

A quarter of an hour passed, she had wept three times,
And a day elapsed, nine times had she shed tears.

The man's age, based on his appearance,
Might be the same as her uncle.

With one more look at him
A few years younger she would become.

With one more look at him in the eyes,
The maiden knew his age was not what his beard showed.

And with one more look at him in the eyes,
She would feel his deep love already…

五

姑娘等了五天,他来了,
依然像从前到这里一样。

姑娘高兴得要向前扑,
心里突然对他恨得入骨:

"你早已忘记这个地方,
今天来,又为哪样?

你要忘记就把这里忘个干净,
别三心二意,把这里当歇脚的地方!"

"姑娘,不是我把这里忘记,
因为我的公务繁忙。

"今天一别不知道哪天再见,
我即将起程去远方!

"如今江对岸有一大片地方正荒旱,
我领衙门的饷,不能袖手一旁。"

"你真这么狠心,把这里忘个干净,

纳西古歌三首
Three Old Folk Songs of the Naxi

V

Not until five days later did the man finally come,
As familiar as the first time he had.

Delighted was the maiden to jump to his breast
While suddenly she felt within an unbearable hatred:

"You have, I guess, long left this place behind,
What is the point of showing up again today?

Why not erase this place out of your mind completely?
Never take this place as somewhere you can stop by!"

"You got me wrong, my dear maiden,
Busy have I been these days.

I am leaving for somewhere far away, and
May not have the chance to see you again!

People across the river are suffering from severe drought,
I am monthly paid and cannot sit back."

"O well, considering everyone but me,

好哇，你就不为别人着想！

"镜子打碎了，能补得圆，
一个人的心碎了又怎么样？

"要走你就快走吧，
不然，我就用棍子赶！"

"姑娘，你怎么这样多心，
姑娘，你怎么不能将我体谅！

"我能见别人病了不救？
我能见别人饿了不伸出手？

"当我离开你是这么难过，
一天仿佛一年那么漫长，

"你像用千根丝扯着我，
可是，我怎敢那么乱想……

"我比你大了十几岁，
这么大的人怎忍心爱个姑娘！"

"快别这样说！快别这样讲！

纳西古歌三首
Three Old Folk Songs of the Naxi

How cruel of you to forget this place!

Broken mirrors can be fixed,
Yet what about a broken-hearted maiden?

Please go away if you made the decision,
Otherwise, blame me not for driving you away!"

"Why would you, my sensitive maiden,
Show any understanding and sympathy to me!

How can I turn a cold shoulder to someone starved?
How can I turn a cold shoulder to someone sick?

You have no idea what I have undergone leaving you,
A day seemed to become a year to endure.

You, since we met, have my heart stolen away,
But any improper thoughts I dare not to have…

How can I, more than ten years older,
Express love to a lovely maiden like you?"

"Do not speak words like that! You know not

你不知道我怎么想你,在不见你的时候。

"我不知道你去救病人回不来,
我不知道你送钱给人家回不来。

"我日日夜夜将你等待,
等你啊,你总不来。

"假若你不爱我,你忍心?
假若我不爱你,心上的乱麻斩不断,理不来。

"快别说你比我多了几岁,
我爱你的不是你的胡须是你的人。

"快别说你比我多了几岁,
我爱你的不是你的胡须是你的心。

"你过去的岁月都藏在你那根斑白的头发里,
我见你那根发,能说你不年轻?

"你把那过去的日子都束在一起,
交给我的,是你一生的爱情;

"年纪大一些的人,日子比别人过得多,

纳西古歌三首
Three Old Folk Songs of the Naxi

How much I have missed you these days.

I had no idea you were away saving people,
I had no idea you were giving people timely help.

Expecting you to come back I have been,
Day after day and night after night.

How could you be so cruel not to love me back?
And why is my life messed up if I love you not.

Do not take your age as the barrier between us,
I have feelings for you and care not about your beard.

Do not take your age as the barrier between us,
Your heart rather than your beard do I care about.

The gray hair tells about the bygone days you had.
How can I call you a lad while I saw your gray hair?

Yet the past you had will, I believe, win me
The love of your entire life.

Your love, I believe, must be deeper than others,

你的爱情，定比别人深沉……"

"姑娘，你尽说些傻话，
年轻人怎么不需要炽烈的爱情？

"我眼看着四十来到，
难道用我迟暮的晚年来送走你的青春！

"那时，你会像在尼姑庵里生活，
那样，我怎么忍心！"

"快别说这些不吉利的话，
说多了，会触怒山神。

"你既然能想到我的终身，
那你爱我的心也一定坚定。

"许多媒人天天上我家门，
只是想用嫁妆来买我的身。

"你爱我，爱得坚定，
你爱我，胜过别人。

"我不爱爱我的人爱哪个？

纳西古歌三首
Three Old Folk Songs of the Naxi

Considering wax and wane experienced at your age…"

"Do not be silly, my dear maiden,
Vigorous love young people also deserve.

Forty I am about to be, I dread to accompany you
In my twilight years while you are in your vigorous youth!

And then how I would bear the thought of you
Living alone by yourself like an old nun!"

"Speak not those unlucky words,
Or the God of Mountains you may offend.

My whole life you have pondered over,
Then your faithfulness to me must be firm too.

Matchmakers have shown up at my door each day,
Only to persuade me with those dowries.

Stable is your love to me,
And unique is your love to me.

Who else should I love back but someone who loves me?

我不爱爱我的人去爱别人?

"你今天就要过金沙江去远方,
此刻是我们要离别的时辰。

"我俩该珍惜这千金的时刻,
别再谈那些恼人的事情!"

六

姑娘和他在江边转了三转,
姑娘和他的情话说个不完。

他要走了,要过江去,
姑娘要他再等一等:

"这次分离不知什么时候见面,
这么匆匆地离去,你怎么忍心!"

"只要这里有乌萨米我就要回来,
最多,也不要你等三年。"

"你说三年的时间还不够长?
离开你就没法过,哪怕是一天!

纳西古歌三首
Three Old Folk Songs of the Naxi

How should I love not the one who cares for me?

You are leaving for somewhere afar across the Jinsha River,
Now it is the time that we should part.

The sad parting we should leave alone for a moment,
And cherish the precious moment together right now!"

VI

The lovely couple wandered along the river,
Speaking and chatting nonstop with each other.

The man, at last, was about to leave,
And the maiden hated to part with him:

"Unknown is the time to meet again,
How can I bear you leaving me so soon?"

"As long as you are here for me,
At most in three years I will come back."

"I cannot live without you for just one day,
Let alone three years expecting you back!

"可是,只要你回来我就要等,
再多等几年,我也不会疲倦。

"此刻,我真不愿想这些事,
好好玩玩吧,在分离的时间!"

他要走了,要过江去,
乌萨米又多留了他一刻。

他要走了,要过江去,
乌萨米又多留他玩了一天。

他俩谈得好亲密,在石洞里边,
他俩在石洞里,别人也看不见。

野花遍地长,也长在石洞中,
每朵野花上,都飞着蜜蜂——

乌萨米偎着他,两个人亲了个嘴,
把两个人的脸都亲得发红。

蜜蜂有了花,蜜蜂长得健壮,
花儿有了蜜蜂,花儿长得美丽;

纳西古歌三首
Three Old Folk Songs of the Naxi

Yet never do I feel tired waiting for you,
As long as you are to return one day.

The precious time upon parting let us enjoy,
And let nothing bother us for the moment!"

Across the river the man was to leave,
Yet a bit longer Wusami asked him to stay.

Across the river the man was about to leave,
Yet another day Wusami begged him to stay.

Inside the cave they were unseen from outside,
Inside the cave an intimate conversation was going on.

Bees were found lighting on wild flowers
Which grew outside as well as inside the cave.

Leaning close to each other, the sweet couple
Kissed on the lips and blushed.

Bees, without flowers, grow not strong,
And flowers, without bees, cease to be beautiful;

古歌 // Old Folk Songs of the Dai & the Naxi

蜜蜂要有花,才能酿蜜,
花儿要蜜蜂浇水,花才生长;

蜜蜂衔了泥放在花树下,
蜜蜂用翅膀驮来水浇在花蕾中——

姑娘像花,他像蜂,
蜂采花,花也戏蜂。①

他玩了一天才过江去,
却留下了一个儿子在乌萨米腹中。

……

七

人要做母亲总是高兴,
乌萨米要做母亲却很痛苦。

乌萨米最讨厌媒人上门来,
要是别人知道她有儿子也不会上她家中。

---

① 以下不雅,故略。

纳西古歌三首
Three Old Folk Songs of the Naxi

Bees, without flowers, make no honey,
And flowers, without bees watering, flourish not either;

Mud carried under the tree came from bees,
And water sprayed on the bud was from bees too.

Flower resembled the maiden and bee the man,
They found each other attractive and congenial.①

After a day spent together, the man left,
Yet Wusami later found herself pregnant with a boy.

......

VII

Having a baby was the happiest thing for women,
Yet Wusami suffered too much to have one.

The last person she wanted to meet was the matchmaker
Who would come not if knowing a baby she carried.

---

① The following part is indecent and deleted.

九十九个男人当中也有好人,
九十九个当中也有人真心爱乌萨米。

只是乌萨米总是一百个、一千个不答应,
乌萨米没出嫁,却有了丈夫。

天天等待自己心爱的男人,
每天等着等着就哭。

父母都气得发怒:
"你什么时候才肯出嫁,要嫁什么样的丈夫?"

"你只要让我再过三年,
到时候你把我嫁什么人都行,

"可是现在你们别迫得我这么紧啊,
生我的、养我的,仁慈的父母!"

等了一年,男家来催婚,
托人家送来九十九双鞋、九十九件衣服。

等到一年,她偷偷地养下儿子,
把儿子送给了砍柴的老公公。

纳西古歌三首
Three Old Folk Songs of the Naxi

Kind people could be found among those 99 men,
And a faithful heart also shown among those 99 men.

Wusami, however, said no to them a thousand times,
Though unmarried, she had had a husband already.

Expecting her beloved to come back,
Wusami spent each day waiting in tears.

Her parents lost patience and questioned:
"Who on earth are you married? And when?"

"Three more years please give me,
Then I will be willing to marry anyone.

And now, my kind parents who gave me precious life,
Please do not force me, in such a rush, to marry."

A man came to propose in a year,
Asking the matchmaker to send 99 pairs of shoes and 99 dresses.

Secretly giving birth to a boy in a year, Wusami had him
Brought up by an old man cutting wood for a living.

等了两年，男家又来催婚，
送来九十九匹马，由乌萨米挑一匹。

男家送来的马，没动她的心，
她也不爱送来的鞋子、衣服……

她一刻要到江边望三遍，
她一天要到江边望九遍。

望一遍回来就哭，
望九遍回来哭得更凶。

眼看着等够三年了，
他，还是没有回来。

一家人都把她围住，
一双双眼都盯着她：

"你约好的三年到期了，
你，还有什么话！

"如今是你嫁也得嫁，
不嫁也得嫁！"

纳西古歌三首
Three Old Folk Songs of the Naxi

Again the man came to propose in two yeas,
Presenting 99 horses for Wusami to choose from.

The maiden showed no interest in the horses and
Neither did she have a feeling for clothes and shoes…

A quarter of an hour passed, three times did Wusami wait by the riverside.
A day elapsed, nine times had she expected her man by the riverside.

Each time the maiden went home in despair and wept,
And at the end of the day she shed tears in sorrow.

Three years were about to pass, yet
Her love was still nowhere to be seen.

No longer sitting still, her parents began
To question what she once promised:

"What else can you say? Three years
You promised have passed!

No matter what bear in your mind now,
You have to keep your words and get married!"

她想说不能说,
她要讲不能讲。

走到江边还不见他来,
只有对着水哭:"天哇!"

八

大道上跑着快马,
江河上走着快船。

爬山越岭,披星戴月,
他赶回来了,赶回来了!

他走了三年零一天,
他才赶回来!

他失约了,
没有照着姑娘约好的日子归来。

姑娘,你等够了吧?
哎,因为遍地遭灾。

他公务在身,抽身不开,

纳西古歌三首
Three Old Folk Songs of the Naxi

Unable to speak back this time,
And hard to explain either.

Wusami cried and yelled
By the riverside where her husband was still not seen.

VIII

Catching up on the horse at full gallop,
And later transferring to water,

The man, after a long trek overnight,
Finally made it back!

One day, however, later after
Three years of what he once promised!

Failed had the man to return the day
He and his maiden had agreed upon.

Did the hopeless waiting break your heart, my dear maiden?
I could not return due to disasters pervading, alas!

Expecting to see his maiden though, he

走不到她身边来。

可是这一次来了,
将永远不和你分开。

去海角,带你去海角,
去天涯,带你上天涯!

只要姑娘不怪他失约,
他愿向她做百个揖,叩百个头。

她怎么治他,他都甘愿,
只要她不说他把她忘怀……

现在他来了,
她怎么不来接他!

一把锁将门把住,
一对嫁女的对联压在门上。

一朵鬓花落在地上,
泪水滴在花蕾中央!

过往一丝甜蜜的回忆,

纳西古歌三首
Three Old Folk Songs of the Naxi

Left not behind those who suffered misery either.

Finally arrived the man this time,
Determining to part no longer from her.

And to bring Wusami with him to
Wherever he was about to go!

As long as the maiden forgave him,
A hundred times he would bow down to her.

As long as the maiden forgot him not,
No matter what punishment he would like to take…

He came now, yet in despair, since
His lovely Wusami was nowhere to be seen!

What the man saw was the locked door
On which a couplet for wedding pasted.

On the ground he found a headdress flower, and
A drop of sad tears seemed still to be seen on the petal!

The sweet memory, alas, with his dear maiden,

如今都化为辛酸!

没赶来,相思叫人心疼,
赶来了,只见人去楼空!

懒洋洋走在分离时住过的石洞,
猛见她留下的字:"赶快!"

赶赶赶,快马又加鞭,
赶赶赶,姑娘,怎样才能把你赶上!

九

来接新娘的人前呼后拥,
人前马后,好不威风。

乌萨米在马上啼啼哭哭,
在马上,坐也坐不住。

马向前走一步,乌萨米回头望三望,
马向前走三步,乌萨米回头望九次。

她男人追在后面唤了她三声,
她在马上没有听见;

纳西古歌三首
Three Old Folk Songs of the Naxi

Had been reduced to something bitter!

Days wore on like years while long separated,
Now the man returned though, his beloved waited no more.

Wandering in despair, the man passed the cave
They used to stay in and saw "hurry up" left on the rock!

Catching up on the horse at full gallop,
The man chased after with all his strength!

IX

Finally came an impressive group of people,
Escorting Wusami back for the wedding.

Unwilling to go with them, the poor maiden
Wept on the horse in such despair.

A step forward on the horse, three times Wusami looked back,
Three steps forward then, nine times Wusami looked back.

The man called her name three times while chasing after her,
Yet failed to get any answer from his beloved maiden;

她男人追在后面唤了她九声,
她在马上还是没有听见。

死水不是养鱼塘,
乌萨米不愿嫁给她不爱的富翁。

鱼儿落在网里回头也不行,
乌萨米再向后望也没有什么用。

新娘子在马上哭,
哭得男家一家大小发怒;

新娘子不断回头望,
望得新郎心里酸得发苦。

这家人骂她一声她哭了,
骂她三声她哭得更苦。

她哭,哭来了一阵妖风,
妖神不准她爱她丈夫。

迎亲的人前扯后拥,
地上滚起了一阵狂风。

纳西古歌三首
Three Old Folk Songs of the Naxi

The man called her name nine times while chasing after her,
Yet failed to get any answer from his beloved maiden still.

Marrying some millionaire Wusami had no feelings for
Would be as painful as keeping fish in dead water.

Yet meaningless was looking back then,
Wusami was like a fish caught in the net.

Seeing Wusami weeping on the horse,
Furious the bridegroom and his family became;

Seeing Wusami looking back now and then,
The bridegroom had his feelings deeply hurt.

Blamed once, Wusami shed tears,
Blamed twice, she wept her heart out.

A burst of evil wind her crying drew on, and
The evil allowed not Wusami to love her husband.

A violent gust of wind came later, and
The escorting entourage could barely stand still.

风卷得黄沙漫天飞舞,
黄沙顿时遮住了太阳,黑了天空。

风沙拍击着天空,
风沙拆散了迎亲的队伍。

天上地下什么也看不见,
只见乌萨米的马还在走动。

忽然它把乌萨米抛在半空,
一只玉鹿在半空把乌萨米接住。

玉鹿一天走十万八千里,
在天上腾云驾雾……

玉鹿带着她走了三天三夜,
依然把她带到她家乡的山峰。

她骑在玉鹿上向前瞭望,
永远在山岩上站立不动。

一只手愤怒地指着金沙江,
水啊,你怎么不飘来她丈夫!

纳西古歌三首
Three Old Folk Songs of the Naxi

Flying in the air, the sand
Covered the sun and darkened the sky.

Impossible to distinguish direction over the flying sand,
The escorts got separated in the dark.

Amidst the flying sand nothing could be seen clearly,
Only the horse carrying Wusami was still walking.

Suddenly up in the air did it throw Wusami and
An immortal deer caught her and ran away.

Riding on the mist and clouds, the deer
Walked the long distance of 108,000 miles a day…

After three days' trekking, Wusami finally
Was brought back to the mountain of her hometown.

Overlooking from the mountain top on the deer,
Wusami stood still on the rock for good.

Pointing to the Jinsha River with rage, she wondered
Why Mother River brought not her beloved!

当她丈夫赶来,她已化成石像,
脸上淌下了泪珠!

丈夫抱来儿子在石像下哭,
乌萨米心动了,身子却不能动。

她丈夫唤她一声,
她心里想回答,嘴却不能动。

丈夫想得他流干了泪,
乌萨米在山上哭干了泪!

她爱着自己的男人和儿子,
更爱着自己的乡土……

每当年成不好,
她总预先告诉自己乡友。

每当春天来到,
她在山上叫着"布谷"。

六个妹妹来约姐玩,
七姐妹的笑声混在一起,分不出。

纳西古歌三首
Three Old Folk Songs of the Naxi

Wusami, when came her husband at last, had became
A figure in stone with tears still to be seen on her face!

Her beloved wept below the statue with their baby,
Wusami wanted to respond yet was unable to move.

Her beloved called her name,
Wusami wanted to answer yet her efforts were in vain.

The man missed his maiden and dried his tears,
So did Wusami, crying aloud inside her heart!

Loving her beloved man and their boy, Wusami
Also showed deep love for her hometown…

If a rough year was to come, she
Informed her dear fellow countrymen beforehand.

Each year when spring was approaching, she
Was singing like a cuckoo over the mountain.

The six younger sisters came to play with her,
And their laughter could not be distinguished from one another.

古歌 // Old Folk Songs of the Dai & the Naxi

她们乐了,她也乐了,
她们笑了,她也笑了。

笑声在山谷里回荡,
播向四面八方……

纳西古歌三首
Three Old Folk Songs of the Naxi

Six sisters were cheerful, she was cheerful too.

Six sisters laughed, she laughed too.

Smiled the six younger sisters, and so did Wusami,

For long echoes of laughter resounded in the valley.

古歌 // Old Folk Songs of the Dai & the Naxi

猎 歌

一

父母养下儿子三个,
分家时,当我九岁时光。

老大生来是一家之长,
老三,分得了租房;

父母不给我钱财,又不让我读书,
九岁起,出外流浪。

过了十八年,我又回来了,
依然背个空空的钱囊……

没有带回荣誉,也没有带回钱财,
依然是个穷光棍汉……

走进家门,痛苦,懊丧,
却带着新的希望……

纳西古歌三首
Three Old Folk Songs of the Naxi

Hunting Song

I

Two brothers had I and when I was nine,
They divided up the family property and lived apart.

Born the master of the house was the oldest,
And the youngest won a house for rent;

Yet only I wandered at the age of nine, with
No support or permission from the family to attend school.

Back was I finally after eighteen years of rootless life,
And no money had been saved in my pocket…

Still a poor wretch was I back home,
Neither honor nor money did I bring back…

Sad and depressed back home though,
A glimmer of hope still stirred inside my heart…

古歌 // Old Folk Songs of the Dai & the Naxi

十八年了,十八年了,
过去的是流水似的时光……

十八年了,儿子穷得像从前一样,
只是多了把胡子和满腹的愁肠。

我知道,这给家里丢尽脸,
没带回荣誉,却像叫花子一样。

可是,这又有什么办法想?
我又是次子,又不会偷抢!

我敲了门,喊着家里人,
希望父母会认儿子,弟弟会认兄长!

可是我敲门,
门里像没有主人一样;

我喊着家里人,
一个个像不认识我一样。

"你不要走错了门,
你的家不在这个地方!"

纳西古歌三首
Three Old Folk Songs of the Naxi

Like an arrow how time flied,
Eighteen years, suddenly, slipped away…

Penniless still as former days was I now,
Yet only with more beard and sadness.

Surely did I know the disgrace I brought back,
Living as a beggar without anything honorable achieved.

Yet what else should I do?
I was the second son who would never steal and loot!

I knocked at the door and called their names,
Hoping someone came to meet this son and brother!

Yet though I kept knocking no matter how hard I try,
No response came as though no one was home;

Calling their names loudly,
No response came as though no one knew me.

"You are going to the wrong door,
Here is not where you belong!" came the voice finally.

"我找了十八年都没有找到家,
我的家该在什么地方?"

"你只有上山才能找到吃的,
你的家,该在那个地方!"

二

山上,深谷接着深谷,
山顶的积雪白茫茫;

松林古树望不到边,
是野兽的家乡!

香鹿、青麂、野兔,
一群群的躲在雪山上。

想走一步,山路崎岖,
想跑一步,悬崖峭壁悬在四方。

春天,没处躲雨,
冬日,没处躲冰雹,

纳西古歌三首
Three Old Folk Songs of the Naxi

"Then where should I head back
After eighteen years of efforts in vain?"

Came the voice again, "go to the mountain
Where you can find food and where you belong!"

II

Deep valleys stretched over the mountain,
Which was capped with heavy snow;

Pine trees in the mountain saw no end,
Where wild animals usually hid and foraged!

Deep in the snow mountain hid
Deer, muntjac, and rabbits.

I felt hard to take each step, let alone run
Along the zigzag mountain trail with cliffs arching around.

Nowhere to hide from the spring rain,
Nor the fierce hailstones in winter.

没有吃的,肚子饥,
没有穿的,身上寒。

我又走下山来,
正当九月的时光,

九月是收获的季节,
我总能找到一些吃的;

九月是收获的季节,
收割后,也许能找到块播种的地方。

是,家里对我依然是那样,
一群人看我用黑眼,一群人看我用白眼:

"你怎么像游魂一样,
游到我们家门上?"

"收留我吧!收留我吧!
看在你们曾养育我的分上!"

"假使你是我们家的儿子,
分家时,为什么不给家里争来光荣!

纳西古歌三首
Three Old Folk Songs of the Naxi

I was starved from scarce food,
And suffered without enough clothes to keep warm.

I went down the hill
Right around September.①

Right at the time of harvest,
So that I could find some food anyway;

Right at the time of harvest,
So that I might find a land to cultivate;

My family treated me as usual
With contemptuous attitudes:

"Why are you haunting us
Like a lingering ghost?"

"Please keep me stay, my dear family,
For the sake of you once bringing me up!"

"Were you our son, you would bring us
Honor during the time of family separation!

---

①The months in the Naxi songs refer to lunar months. —Translator's note.

"假若你是我们家的儿子,
你这个样子,怎么还有脸回家乡!

"走吧!你的命注定你只能在山上,
去播种,你自己去开荒!"

我走出门口,只有猎犬送我,
舔着我,看着我,用那悲哀的眼光。

哎,猎犬啊,坏了心的人还不如你,
你还没把你的主人遗忘!

他们也赶你!他们有钱就不打猎了,
你啊,还是跟我一同去山上……

三

山上依然无法生活,
可是我死也不再下山。

大雪山,分三重,
重重雪山,重重高峰,

纳西古歌三首
Three Old Folk Songs of the Naxi

"Were you our son, you would not bear the shame
Of going back home upon living a penniless life.

You would better leave for the mountain
Where you can cultivate land on your own!"

I left in despair with only the hunting dog
Licking and looking at me sadly.

My hound, alas, remembered its master still,
Yet people with blood relations did not!

They hunted no more as they became rich,
Come with me to the mountain, my dear hound…

III

Hard was the mountain life though,
I decided to settle down no matter what.

High and steep were the snow mountains,
Mountains beyond mountains stretching endlessly.

山坡大,猛兽凶,
要上山,困难重重。

恨我穷,买不起糍粑,
饿着肚子,哪有力气爬上最高峰。

想上二重山啊,
又有凶恶的山神把守在山上,

想上二重山得先敬山神,
没有钱,怎能将神祭响!

三重山,路途短,
密林深处的小路通向四方。

遍山的丛林,遍山的藤蔓,
青草也在遍山长,

麂子在青草里叫,
白鹿在山上乱跑,

我想上第三重山去打猎,
可是又没有火枪?

纳西古歌三首
Three Old Folk Songs of the Naxi

The steep mountain with wild animals prowling
Must be difficult to be climbed to the top.

Unfortunate was it that I cannot afford to buy ciba①,
How could I have strength to summit the mountain?

Half way up the hill I expected to reach,
Yet the fierce mountain god safeguarded it.

I could not afford to worship the mountain god,
Half way up the hill how I could reach!

Finally, not far away was the mountain top,
And paths deep down the woods led to all directions.

All over the mountain grew vines and grass
Which made the path towards the summit tougher.

Muntjac were barking in the green grass,
And deer leaping on the mountain.

Expecting to hunt on the mountain top,
Yet a shotgun I did not have.

---

① A traditional Chinese cuisine of cooked glutinous rice pounded into paste. —Translator's note

我想上第三重山去打猎，
没人引路，小路通向何方？

哦，大鹰来了，向我飞来了！
它在前面走，是为我引路。

哦，我的猎犬来到身旁，
有它，顶上一枝火枪……

四

山上的日子过得好孤寂，
像喇嘛在庙里一样……

遍山是密麻麻的树，
我却找不到伙伴！

遍山是泉水和风，
它们又怎么能和我做伴！

孤零的日子真难过啊，
男人怎能缺少女人的温暖；

纳西古歌三首
Three Old Folk Songs of the Naxi

Expecting to hunt on the mountain top,

Yet no one showed me the way in the front.

O an eagle was flying to me,

Leading my way to the destination!

O my hound was coming to my side,

He was my bodyguard…

IV

Solitary was the life on the mountain,

As monks living in the temple…

I had no one accompanying me,

But trees dotting over the mountain!

I had no one accompanying me

But springs and howling wind around my ears!

Solitude was the last thing I can conquer,

Without the care of my love how I could survive;

古歌 // Old Folk Songs of the Dai & the Naxi

我想下山去娶个妻子,
可是我发誓再也不下山;

我想娶个妻子来安家,
谁又会嫁给我这穷光棍汉!

我跑遍了整个山,
如今只有这条猎犬在我身旁。

它耳朵尖,眼睛亮,
再好的猎犬也比不上。

早上我吃野果,
还能有什么喂它?

晚上打猎回来,
只能给它一碗野味汤。

可是上山打猎它走先,
淌河过水它蹲在岸上。

白天它会打猎还会剥狐狸皮,
晚上它和我一同睡在篝火旁。

纳西古歌三首
Three Old Folk Songs of the Naxi

I had sworn not to return down the hill,
Otherwise a soul mate I would find in my life;

Yet who would like to be my soul mate,
Marrying some penniless bachelor like me!

I ran over the mountain with only
My hound staying by my side.

No dog surpassed my dear hound
With sensitive ears and sharp eyes.

O what else could I feed him in the morning,
Except wild fruits I only had?

O what else could I feed him at night,
Except soup of the wild animal hunted?

He always led the way ahead,
And carried me across the river.

Hunting and skinning fox in the daytime,
The hound slept beside me by the fire at night.

小猎犬成了我的朋友,
小猎犬成了我的伙伴。

每天我握着桑木弓,
背上了雕翎箭。

猎犬就在前面跑了,
我们打猎在林间和溪旁……

五

野花,遍山开放,
我们走在林荫道上。

小猎犬,竖直了耳朵在听,
小猎犬,翘起了鼻孔在闻,

小猎犬,狂吠一阵,
跳过山涧,奔进树林。

马鹿在前面跑,
猎犬在后面紧跟。

马鹿在前面忙着逃命,

纳西古歌三首
Three Old Folk Songs of the Naxi

My friend the little hound had become,
My companion the little hound had become.

Each day I took the bow made from mulberry tree,
And carried arrows with eagle feathers.

The hound ran in front,
In the woods and by the brook we hunted…

V

We appreciated the blooming flowers all over the mountain
While going out for a stroll on the lane.

Suddenly, my dear hound pricked up its ears,
And tilted up its nose to smell something.

Barking wildly for a while, the hound
Leaped over the stream and rushed into the woods.

The hound was chasing closely after
A red deer running in front.

In front the red deer escaped,

猎犬在后面狂吠一阵。

马鹿跑得快，
猎犬追得紧；

马鹿跳三跳，
猎犬吠九声；

马鹿跑得快，
猎犬追得紧；

钻进深草，穿过森林，
老林里啊，愈走愈深。

只见老林里黑压压的一片，
只听见风吹落叶的声音……

哦，看不见马鹿的踪影！
也听不见猎犬的吠声，

想去追马鹿啊，
前面的雪山层层。

要想找回小猎犬啊，

纳西古歌三首
Three Old Folk Songs of the Naxi

While the hound barked and chased behind.

Faster and faster the deer ran,
And nonstop the hound chased after it;

Three times the red deer leapt in front,
While the hound barked nine times behind;

Faster and faster the deer ran,
And nonstop the hound chased after it;

Into the deep grass and through the woods,
And deeper and deeper the woods had become.

Nothing but darkness was what I saw in the forest,
Nor did I hear anything but the sound of drifting leaves…

Suddenly, alas, I saw not the red deer,
Nor did I hear the barking of my hound!

I expected to chase the red deer, yet failed
Due to the steep mountain blocking my way.

I expected to find the little hound,

哪里是去找它的路哩?

小猎犬啊,小猎犬啊,
快回来,回到我身边!

小猎犬啊,小猎犬,
叫你为什么不答应!

我在山上哭泣,
我好悲伤啊,好孤零,

我在山上哭泣,
像失去了亲人!

每天,猎犬在前面将路引,
如今,前面的道路看不明。

我上山,猎犬还跟在我身边,
如今下山,只有我一个人……

六

下山下到半山腰,
遇见一位砍柴的老人:

纳西古歌三首
Three Old Folk Songs of the Naxi

Yet knew not where to head.

My dear hound, alas, please
Come to my side!

My dear hound, alas, why
Did you not answer my call!

Weeping alone on the mountain,
I had sorrow and loneliness accompanying me.

Weeping alone on the mountain,
I felt like losing one family member in the world!

The hound had led my way each day,
Yet now I saw not clearly the way ahead.

Still with me was the hound yesterday,
Yet now only solitude accompanied me…

VI

I met an old man collecting firewood
Half way down the mountain:

古歌 // Old Folk Songs of the Dai & the Naxi

"老伯,劳问您一声,
你可见一只猎犬追马鹿?

"我今天出猎倒霉得很,
东西没打着,倒不见猎犬的踪影!"

樵夫赶忙回答:
"我上山砍柴已整整一日,

"只听见风吹落叶飒飒地响,
只听见溪水和搅拌山风的声音。

"我没有看见有猎犬从这里走过,
更不见猎犬追马鹿的形影!"

唉,我呼唤我的猎犬,
只有风在答应。

我的心里充满了泪水,
像一江春水翻滚。

我走下山,心中郁闷,
迎面走来了个牧羊人:

纳西古歌三首
Three Old Folk Songs of the Naxi

"Excuse me, Sir, have you seen
A hound chasing a deer today?

I had a bad day hunting today,
Losing my dear hound with nothing gained!"

Answered the old man, "I have collected
Firewood on the mountain all day long,

Yet I saw not the hound running by,
Nor did I find the hound chasing a deer.

I only heard the whisper of the drifting leaves, and
The trickling stream with the mountain breeze."

I called my dear hound,
Yet only the sound of wind replied.

Suffering from the pain of loss,
My heart filled with an ocean of tears.

Depressed as I went down the mountain,
And saw a shepherd walking towards me:

"牧羊的大哥,劳问一声,
你可见一只猎犬追马鹿?

"我今天出猎倒霉得很,
东西没打着,倒不见猎犬的踪影!"

牧羊人赶忙回答我:
"我上山,赶着羊群,

"只见弯弯的羊角在拨动青草,
只听见羊儿吃草的'唰唰'声。

"我没有看见有猎犬从这里去过,
更不见猎犬追马鹿的形影!"

我走下山,山顶的白雪刺眼睛,
送我回家的,只有山风一阵又一阵,

上山时,猎犬跟在我身边,
下山来,孤单单的一个人……

我依然一无所有,
像次子的命注定就是这样;

纳西古歌三首
Three Old Folk Songs of the Naxi

"Excuse me, Sir, have you seen

A hound chasing a deer today?

I had a bad day hunting today,

Losing my dear hound with nothing gained!"

Answered the shepherd right away:

"I drifted the herds up the mountain today,

I saw only sheep horns stirring the grass,

And heard grass being chewed.

Yet I saw not the hound running by,

Nor did I find the hound chasing a deer!"

Dazzling my eyes was the snow-capped peak,

While nothing but a gust of wind walked me home.

Up the mountain the hound used to accompany me,

Yet down the hill I was all by myself now…

I lost everything, as it was fated to be

The destiny of the second son in the family;

古歌 // Old Folk Songs of the Dai & the Naxi

我依然一无所有，
像被赶出家门的时候一样。

哎，这样的日子什么时候完？
这样的日子还得有多长？

七

雪山下是玉湖池，
山上青青的松林倒映在水中。

山顶的积雪，天上的白云，
仿佛在水面漂浮……

有个姑娘在池边，
捣碎了池中的水影……

我饥渴，我愁闷，
我，慢慢走近水滨。

我要喝完池中的水，
才能解我的渴；

纳西古歌三首
Three Old Folk Songs of the Naxi

I lost everything, like the scene of being
Kicked out of my family was staged again;

Alas! How long should I bear the penniless life?
And how long should I bear the life of solitude?

VII

Under the foot of the Snow Mountain is Jade Lake,
Where reflections of green pine trees can be seen.

Snows on the mountain peak and the white clouds
Over the sky seemed to be floating on the lake…

By the lake stood a beautiful girl,
Disturbing the reflections in the lake…

Disappointed though, I approached the lake
Intending to quench my thirst and satisfy my hunger.

The thirst, I am afraid, might not be quenched
Unless I drank all the water the lake contains;

我，要喝完池中的凉水，
才能止住心中的烦闷。

我低头饮着清凉的池水，
雪山在眼前，姑娘在身边。

哦，马鹿，马鹿，
从倒映在水中的松林跳出。

小猎犬在马鹿后面紧追，
马鹿跳三跳，猎犬吠九声。

我跳起来，跑着向前，
张开桑木弓，搭上雕翎箭。

面对面也射来一箭，
哦，白鹿倒在雪崖边……

小猎犬啊，小猎犬，
你又回到我身边。

你摇头摆尾伏在我跟前，
你伸着舌头，将我的脚跟舔。

纳西古歌三首
Three Old Folk Songs of the Naxi

And the sadness inside my heart might be eliminated
Only if I drank all the water the lake contains.

With the mountain in front and the maiden beside,
I lowered myself down and drank the water from the lake.

The deer, all of a sudden, leaped out of the woods
Seen from the reflection in the lake.

Chasing behind was my dear hound,
Barking and running after closely.

Jumping up immediately, I ran after,
Preparing to shoot the deer with my bow.

Yet suddenly an arrow was shot from the opposite side,
And the deer fell by the cliff…

My dear hound, dear hound,
Finally returned to my side.

Crouching in front of me wagging its tail,
The hound kept licking my heel.

你这样,是离我太久?
你这样,是要讨我喜欢?

可是你为什么只谢我?
还不快去姑娘跟前!

是她将马鹿射死,
只有她,才值得你讨她喜欢。

你看她那双秀眼,
你看她漫步湖边。

你看她双脚轻轻地向前移动,
仿佛要来到我跟前。

我真想上前去谢她一声,
为她刚刚射出的那一箭。

去吧,小猎犬,去舔她的脚,
就像伏在我的身边。

八

小猎犬,鹿皮我用刀割,

纳西古歌三首
Three Old Folk Songs of the Naxi

Did you miss me out there these days?
Or just try to gain affections from me?

Yet not enough was it to thank me solely, my hound,
The maiden you should give thanks to! Hurry up!

She shot the deer to death so that you could return to me,
And she surely was the one you should gain affection from.

With bright eyes that seemed to speak, the maiden
Wandered all alone by Jade Lake.

Moving slowly forward, the fair maiden
Seemed to come to my side.

Express gratitude to her I truly intended to,
For the timely arrow she just shot.

Dear hound, please go to lick her feet
Just as what you did to me before.

VIII

With a knife I cut the deer skin,

鹿肉我用火烤；

鹿茸，我揣在怀里，
鹿心血，我装在小瓶中，

可是，鹿肉虽然又香又嫩，
这样的山珍，却没有客人可请！

鹿皮只能作女披肩却没有人缝，
缝好了也没有哪个姑娘可送！

小猎犬，我请你吃鹿肉，
小猎犬，我请你吃鹿筋。

可是你要把鹿皮送给她作披肩，
要把她请来作我们的客人。

说我要请她喝鹿心血啊，
说我要向她倾吐千言万语。

说世上没有人像她那样爱过我，
哪怕她那一箭，只为对我怜悯。

说世上没有人像她那样爱过我，

纳西古歌三首
Three Old Folk Songs of the Naxi

And with fire I cooked its meat;

In my pocket I put the precious antlers,
And filled my bottle with the blood of the deer heart.

A delicious delicacy of the tender meat though,
A great shame was it that no one came to join us!

Perfect was the deer skin for a lady's shawl, yet no one sewed,
And who was going to wear the shawl sown anyway?

My dear hound, venison I invited you to eat,
My dear hound, sinew meat I invited you to taste.

Yet invite the maiden, please, to come to our house,
And present her the deer skin as a shawl.

Ask her to come drink the blood of the deer heart,
And tell her I am pouring out my heart to her.

Tell her no one cares for me like she did in the world,
Even though out of sympathy was the timely arrow shot.

Tell her no one cares for me like she did in the world,

我一生到世上，就这么孤零。

我不管她为什么射出那一箭，
不管她是帮助我，还是她也是猎人。

我不管她为什么射出那一箭，
那一箭，却已射中我的心……

假若她只是为了帮我射死马鹿，
可是像她这样的人，我一生还没遇过第二个。

假若她只是为了怜悯我，
孤零的人，更需要她的温存。

我请她来喝鹿心血，
鹿心血会使两颗心变成一颗心；

鹿心血会驱散我们的烦闷，
鹿心血会使我们永不离分；

鹿心血会使我们永远年轻，
鹿心血会使爱情更加甜蜜。

要她来喝啊，要她来喝啊，

纳西古歌三首
Three Old Folk Songs of the Naxi

Since solitude had been accompanying my entire life.

Out of her instinct of help or the duty of a hunter,
I cared not why she shot the timely arrow.

I cared not why she shot the timely arrow,
Since the arrow she shot had stolen my heart…

In my entire life I had not met a kind person like her,
Even if helping me capture the deer was all she aimed to do.

I cared not if she did it out of sympathy, since
Longing for her tender care was what lonely people do.

Inviting her to enjoy the blood of the deer heart,
Which might bring our hearts closer further;

The blood of the deer heart would dispel sadness,
And keep us separated no more for the rest of our lives.

The blood of the deer heart would keep us young forever,
And bring a sweet romantic relationship between us.

Invite her, my dear hound, to taste

古歌 // Old Folk Songs of the Dai & the Naxi

那不是鹿心血,那是爱情的酒!

尽情喝啊、尽情喝啊,
爱情的酒,不会醉人;

酒使你醉了爱情,
你的心,也永远清醒!

小猎犬,你快请她来,
姑娘,我的心也已向你飞奔——

玉湖池中的水深,
我心比池中的水深;

玉龙雪山的峰顶高,
我的心高过玉龙雪山的峰顶;

千言万语我说不出一句,
我也要陪她坐到天明;

即使她一百个、一千个不答应,
我对她也永远忠诚;

去吧,猎犬,去吧,猎犬,

纳西古歌三首
Three Old Folk Songs of the Naxi

The blood of the deer heart, the wine of love!

Please enjoy the wine of love,
The wine of love shall not make you drunk;

Even if you were drunk in front of love,
Forever your heart should stay awake!

Invite her to come join us, my little hound,
I could not wait to meet her already.

Bottomless was the deep water from Jade Lake,
Yet deeper was my heartfelt feelings for her;

Towering was the peak of the Jade Dragon Snow Mountain,
Yet higher was my heartfelt feelings for her;

Too nervous to speak a word to her even though,
I would rather accompany her all night long;

Eternally I would show my loyalty only to her,
Even though she rejected me a thousand times;

Run, my dear hound, run,

古歌 // Old Folk Songs of the Dai & the Naxi

你快走,你飞奔!

你为我请来贵客!
也为你请来自己的女主人!

说我要同她并肩歌唱,
我要和她一同对饮。

鹿心血会使爱情甜蜜,
使爱情甜蜜的,是互相忠诚。

她要是怕我抱紧她,
我就不抱紧她;

她要是怕我亲她,
我就不吻。

只要她来到我的身边,
只要她来到我的身边;

爹娘不要的人有人爱,
孤零的人也不再孤零。

猎犬啊,你快走,

纳西古歌三首
Three Old Folk Songs of the Naxi

Go and invite the girl to come!

Someone important was the maiden you were to invite,
And the hostess of our house you were to invite!

Tell her I would like to sing with her,
Tell her I would like to drink with her.

Drinking with her the blood of the deer heart, which,
Along with mutual honesty, would harvest a sweet love.

Hug her tightly I would not, if
She showed any reluctance;

Kiss her I would not, if
She showed any reluctance still;

Whatever she pleased I would do,
Only if by my side she stayed forever.

Unloved no more I would become,
Desolate no more I would come to be.

Come on, my dear hound,

去为我请来贵宾,

猎犬啊,你快走,
去请来你的女主人……

纳西古歌三首
Three Old Folk Songs of the Naxi

Go and invite the important guest;

Come on, my dear hound,

Go and invite the hostess of our house…

古歌 // Old Folk Songs of the Dai & the Naxi

游 悲

一

女：
"哎，我能咒怨谁呀！
我能咒怨生长我的地方？

"哎，我能咒怨谁呀！
我能咒怨我的爹娘？

"哎，我能咒怨谁呀！
我能咒怨我自己？

"我啊，是有苦难言，
我啊，是奇痛难当。

"我要吹口弦啊，
口弦吹不尽我的忧伤。

"我要对个人说啊，

纳西古歌三首
Three Old Folk Songs of the Naxi

Sad Wandering Song

I

Female:
"What else, alas, should I blame!
Ridiculous is it to resent the land where I grew up.

Who else, alas, should I blame!
Ridiculous is it to resent my dear parents.

Who else, alas, should I blame!
Ridiculous is it to resent nobody but myself.

Unspeakable is what I have suffered,
And unbearable is what I have been enduring.

In vain was I trying to let go of sadness
Through playing my favorite jaw harp.

I wonder who has the mercy to

古歌 // Old Folk Songs of the Dai & the Naxi

谁又有慈悲的心肠?

"谁怜悯我也救不了我,
那种怜悯,又有什么用场?

"哎,我唱又有什么用?
可是我偏偏想唱。

"可是唱不成了,唱不成了,
世上没有我唱的时间;

"唱不成了,唱不成了,
世上没有我活下去的地方。

"哦,妈呀,妈呀,
你教我用剪刀剪布裁衣裳,

"可是我没纱织布呀,
也没人给我买布做衣裳。

"哦,囡的妈呀!
你教我用绳子背东西,

"我只给你背来一身债啊,

纳西古歌三首
Three Old Folk Songs of the Naxi

Listen attentively to my sorrow.

And in vain was I replying on mercy
Which I think was useless too.

Pointless is my singing right now,
Yet singing loudly is just what I want to do.

The shame is there is no time left in the world
For me to sing to my heart's content.

The shame is there is nowhere else I could settle down,
Let alone sing to my heart's content.

My dear mama, alas, once you have taught me
To tailor cloth and make clothes with scissors.

Yet now the yarn for cloth weaving I own not,
Let alone the cloth do I need for making clothes.

My dear mama, alas, once you have taught me
To carry stuff with a rope.

Yet I carried today not money and valuables,

没给你背来财宝、银两。

"哦,囡的妈呀,
你教我用药毒老鼠,

"我自己都攒不下隔天的米,
哪里有它吃的粮?

"可是,现在啊,
剪刀我有用了。

"绳索我有用了,
毒药我有用了。

"我不用剪刀裁衣裳,
我不用绳索背宝箱。

"老鼠不来我房里,
老鼠也不会死在我手上。

"我活不成了,
前面只有一条路。

"我活不成了,

纳西古歌三首
Three Old Folk Songs of the Naxi

But a heavy debt laid on the family.

My dear mama, alas, once you have taught me
To get rid of rats with poison.

Yet how could rats show up at my home
Where food for the next day was my major concern?

At present, however, a good use
Of the scissor I have found.

At present, however, a good use
Of the rope and poison I have found.

To tailor clothes I use not the scissor,
And to carry treasure I use not the rope.

Rats show up not in my room,
And rats die not by my hand.

In front of me I see only one path
Which leads me to nowhere but the underworld.

There is no place for me in the world,

世上也没我生长的地方！"

二

男：

"唉，你为什么那样想，
你就不留恋生长你的家乡？

"雪山上的积雪闪亮，
漆黑的夜里天上都像有月光。

"六月，雪山上吹下凉风，
腊月，寒风大山抵挡。

"化下的雪水好解渴啊，
化下的雪水像面镜子一样。

"田里没放下犁刀，
泥土就翻开了波浪。

"种下谷种去，
就不用担心收成怎样。

"牡鹿常常跑下山来，

纳西古歌三首
Three Old Folk Songs of the Naxi

Who ends up nowhere but the underworld!"

II

Male:
"Alas, what makes you think that way?
Can you bear to part with your motherland?

The snow-capped mountain top sparkles,
Lighting the night sky like moonlight does.

Cool breeze blows from the snow mountain in June,
And in winter the mountain wards off the freezing wind.

Perfect is the melting snow-water to quench thirst,
And to look at as a natural mirror while dressing.

A coulter is still nowhere to be seen in the field,
Yet the soil has already been cultivated like waves.

Worry not about the harvest of the coming year
Once the corn seeds are sowed in the land.

Stags are often seen wandering at the foot of the mountain,

古歌 // Old Folk Songs of the Dai & the Naxi

老鹰总是盘旋在山顶上。

"泉水从地层中冒了出来,
冲击着石板,急湍地流淌。

"姑娘不需要买镜子呀,
对着泉水就能梳妆。

"圆顶帽①照在水里,黑缎发亮,
长发照在水里,像乌云一样。

"百褶裙照在水里分外好看,
微波荡漾的水啊,也像裙褶一样。

"小姑娘在水里照照都害羞了,
她发现水波映得自己分外漂亮……

"姑娘要托水捎封信,
它会把她的心意捎给情郎。

"你要是喝过一口这里的水啊,
也一定会舍不得这个地方。"

---

① 从前纳西族妇女都戴圆顶帽,这种帽子有的地方称瓜皮帽。

纳西古歌三首
Three Old Folk Songs of the Naxi

And eagles hovering above the mountain peak.

Emerging from the earth, the spring
Flows rapidly and strikes the slate.

And it becomes the perfect natural mirror
For fair maidens dressing and making up.

Reflections from the water display a rounded-top hat[①],
And the long and jet-black hair of the fair maiden.

Also lovely is the maiden's pleated skirt reflected in the water,
Making it hard to distinguish the skirt furbelow from the ripple.

The fair maiden turned pink with blush discovering
Her charming face reflected in the water…

Sending a love letter to her beloved via water,
The maiden would pour out all her feelings of love.

Anyone, once drinking the spring water, would
Surely be reluctant to depart from this land."

---

① In the past, Naxi women wore rounded-top hats which were called watermelon hat by them.

古歌 // Old Folk Songs of the Dai & the Naxi

女：

"唉，这里的天是好。
这里的地是好。

"这里的水是好。
这里的人是好。

"姐妹们的山歌唱得响，
河里的水流得长。

"谷子在这里长得好啊，
娃娃在这里养得胖。

"地里都长甜心菜，
苦心菜只有我一个。

"妈妈生下我的第一天，
大家都说我是赔钱货——

"准备好的爆竹不放了，
准备好的酒不请了。

"在我满月的时候，
家里关起门来过，

纳西古歌三首
Three Old Folk Songs of the Naxi

Female:
"Fine is the weather here,
And fertile is the land too.

Clear is the water here,
And kind are the people too.

Clear and loud are folk songs sung here,
And merrily flows the water in the river.

A fine growth of grain here
Feeds our children well.

On the ground grows the sweetheart cabbage,
Which I taste still bitter yet.

Disappointed and cursing was everyone the day
When I, a baby girl, was born to the world.

Unlit were prepared firecrackers for the celebration,
And no one was invited to the prepared feast.

The family kept me cooped up in the house
When I was only one month old.

一家人都骂我，咒我，
狠毒的话啊，好当满月酒喝。

"爹妈养我到五岁，
就要我下地干活，

"说我赚不到嫁妆钱，
看我怎么在婆妈手下过。①

"五岁的囡做不了活，
我只有坐在门外哭啊。

"五岁的囡做不了活，
我只恨自己是女的啊。

"长到七岁爹妈给我七分力气，
割草的竹筐还高过我。

"割了一炷香的时间，
一筐草还割不够。

---

① 从前纳西女人要带许多嫁妆上男家，并要以自己劳动得来的钱养丈夫一生，否则无法在男家生活。

纳西古歌三首
Three Old Folk Songs of the Naxi

And gifts presented that day were nothing
But cruel cursing and swearing at me.

At the age of only five years old,
I was asked to do manual work.

Threatened that without money to buy the dowry,
A hard life I would live with my future mother-in-law.①

Yet except for crying helplessly at the doorway,
What could a five-year-old little girl do?

A five-year old deserved not a life like this,
Yet the destiny was fated the day of her birth.

How should I, at the age of seven,
Carry a crate that was taller than me?

Though an incense burned out,② the crate
Was still not filled up with grass mowed.

---

① In the past, Naxi women had to bring large dowries to her husband's house and make money to support the whole family in her entire life. Otherwise, she would be kicked out of the house.
② In the past, the time passed was often measured by burning incenses. —Translator's note

"背着大半筐草回来,
喂牲口还喂不够。

"草喂牲口喂不够,
妈白眼看我,大声骂我。

"细竹竿抽囡抽得痛啊,
说我偷懒、不做活。

"囡的妈呀,我割不满一篮草,
是你只给七岁的囡七分力气呀!"

三

女:
"唉,我一岁一岁长成人,
苦痛一年比一年深。

"我有苦不能说出自己的苦,
眼泪只能往肚里流。

"我说话,说我嘴长,
我拿针,说我手笨。

纳西古歌三首
Three Old Folk Songs of the Naxi

Finally, I carried back an almost full crate of grass,
Which was still not enough to feed the cattle.

With contempt mama scolded me for
Not bringing back enough grass for the cattle.

With bamboo sticks mama beat me cruelly,
Punishing, as to her words, my laziness.

However, my dear mama, how could
A seven-year old manage the work of a nine-year old?"

III

Female:
"Growing up year after year,
Yet more and more I have suffered.

Unspeakable is what I endure now,
And I dare not to shed tears in front of others.

I was criticized for impolitely intruding when speaking,
And scolded for clumsiness while sewing.

"天不亮我出去做活,
还怕人说我出去太晚,

"天黑我回来还说太早,
其实,外面已满天星星。

"囡的妈呀,
你可做过人家的女儿呀?

"囡的妈呀,
你可知道做囡的苦情?

"你是不是也是这样做人家的囡呀?
你是不是做囡时没有什么苦情?

"可是人说我们世世代代都是这样啊,
只要你是一个女人!

"女的,就要这样过日子,
女的,就要这样度过一生。

"连天井的石头都要欺侮你,
连门上的门槛都要欺侮你。

纳西古歌三首
Three Old Folk Songs of the Naxi

Before daybreak I got up and worked,
Still fearing the bad name of laziness.

Not until the approach of the dark night with stars over the sky
Did I come back bearing still the accusations of others.

My dear mama, alas, had you not been
Once the daughter of grandma?

My dear mama, alas, had you not once
Experienced the bitterness of being a daughter?

Did you know the same miseries I suffered
Or were you lucky to be a happy daughter?

Yet why was I told that it was the destiny
Of women the day when they were born!

Women are supposed to suffer,
And live in misery for their entire life.

Even courtyard stones and the threshold
Would throw a contemptuous face at me.

"就是死了啊,
也只是个冤魂。

"唉,苦哇,苦啊,
我犯过什么罪?做了什么坏事情?

"我一生下来只是受苦啊,
受苦的只有更深的苦痛是她的报应?

"受苦的人就没有希望?
只有在痛苦中愈陷愈深!

"哦,天啊,天啊!
你为什么不睁开眼睛!

"哦,天啊,天啊,
你对女人为什么这样不公平!

"我白天去砍柴,
砍回来一筐伤心藤,

"藤梗烧成灰烬,
我还是止不住自己的伤心。

纳西古歌三首
Three Old Folk Songs of the Naxi

Women, leaving for the underworld,

Still end up as wandering ghosts.

What a miserable life, alas, I am suffering,

Something bad I might have done in my previous life.

The tough time endured since the day of birth,

I wonder, was what I deserved because of karma.

Why did people in suffering see no hope?

Why were they instead buried deeper and deeper in misery!

My dear lord, alas,

Open your eyes please!

My dear lord, alas,

Why not treat women fairly!

I collected firewood in the daytime,

Yet harvested nothing but sadly a crate of vines.

Burning all the vines to ashes still failed

To alleviate my inner sadness.

"我晚上在挑水,
担回来一担伤心泪,

"那泉眼像我的眼睛,
泪呀流呀,永远流不尽。

"我想好好地哭出自己的伤心泪,
我怕家里说我哭霉了家里的财气。

"我想好好同别人说一说,
可是去找谁说哩?

"找那没有苦处的人,
他不会了解我的苦处;

"找那心里也苦的人,
两人会愈说愈伤心!"

四

男:
"哎,你这样叹息,
唱歌唱得悲凄凄。

纳西古歌三首
Three Old Folk Songs of the Naxi

I carried water at night, yet
Brought back nothing but sad tears.

The source of the spring resembled my eyes,
Shedding its tears endlessly.

How I wish to cry out loud, yet fear that
Tears might drive away good luck from the family.

How I wish to vent my grievances to others,
Yet nobody has come to my mind.

Those who never suffered might know not
What I have been enduring right now;

And those who suffered too might become
Sadder while listening to my woes!"

IV

Male:
"The sorrowful song sang out loud
Miseries you had been enduring.

"它，催得我流泪，
流个不停休。

"急风一吹，枯草折断，
悲歌一唱，疼在我心。

"在这有月亮的晚上，灯光也明亮，
你为什么唱得我断肝肠？

"水泉有水往外冒，
你有伤心话就赶快讲。

"孤雁在秋天找不到方向，
有伤心话的人，你在什么地方？

"你是不是和我一样，
有伤心话没处讲！

"你是不是和我一样，
爹不愿要，娘不愿养！

"你是不是和我一样，
世上没地方立足啊，姑娘！"

纳西古歌三首
Three Old Folk Songs of the Naxi

It made me weep and
Tears could not be held back.

Broken off was the withered grass by a gust of wind,
Just like my fragile heart was grieved by your sad singing.

Broken-hearted was I by your singing
On such a wonderful moonlit night.

I am all ears to any grievances
You would like to pour out.

Have you lost your life direction as
That of the lonely wild goose falling behind.

Have you sunk into the same plight as me,
And found nobody else to turn to?

Have you sunk into the same plight as me,
And have no family to rely on?

Have you sunk into the same plight as me,
And have nowhere else to run from reality?"

女：

"哦，你是南山的青年，
你的家在南庄。

"听说你是个独子，
有什么可悲伤？

"家里人种谷为防饥，
你爹妈养你为防老。

"他们还要你养孙子，
把他的根接上。

"他们二老死了，
还要你做孝子哭丧。

"唉，你还哭什么，
爹妈爱你还不是像金子一样！

"也不知道哪家姑娘嫁给你，
像供尊菩萨把你供起。

"你如今坐在这里吹锦笛，
故意吹得这么悲凄。

纳西古歌三首
Three Old Folk Songs of the Naxi

Female:

"Coming from South Mountain,
You live in South Village.

What on earth should sadden you since
You are the only son in your family.

Like rice grown for feeding people,
Parents raise you for future caretaking.

The family line they also expect you to carry,
Hoping you to have your own children.

When they leave for the underworld one day,
They will rely on their dutiful son to cry at the funeral.

I doubt, alas, that a person adored by parents like gold
has anything to be saddened over!

Anyone who is lucky to marry you would
Cherish you as much as they do Buddha.

Unexpectedly, however, you are sitting here
Playing such a sad song on your flute.

古歌 // Old Folk Songs of the Dai & the Naxi

"好自在的男子汉呀,
你吃了没事,四处可游逛。

"为什么,为什么这样戏弄我,
叫我为你难受一场!"

男:
"现在是有太阳没有光,
我是男子汉又有什么用场!

"我不是独子啊,
不像你说的那样。

"爹妈生下儿子三个,
老天把我排在第二位上。

"老大继承父亲的掌家权,
是一家的家长。

"老三父母都疼爱,
分到一大批家当。

"我有爹妈、兄弟,

纳西古歌三首
Three Old Folk Songs of the Naxi

What a free and comfortable man,
Wandering about without anything to do.

Tricking me into believing and being saddened
By how unfortunate you are as me!"

Male:
"Living in a desperate world without hope to be seen,
What is the point of being a man anyway?

I am not what you have expected,
The precious only child in the family.

Two brothers have I in the family,
Whereas the unlucky second son am I.

The master of the house is the oldest son,
Since he took the role of father under the roof.

Adored by the parents is the youngest,
Inheriting a considerable sum of the family fortune.

Though parents and brothers I do have,

古歌 // Old Folk Songs of the Dai & the Naxi

却跟没有家一样。①

"一家人满肚子私心,
我在家就像外人一样。

"官家要派差,
我就是头牲口,去抵挡。

"这回他们犯了罪,
还要把我当替死鬼当罪犯送上!

"当次子就是这么苦命,
我为什么不悲伤?

"当次子还不如牛马,
当次子还不如做爹妈的囡。

"当囡的只是苦熬几年,
公婆死了,还能把家当。

"可是当次子的啊,
一生还有什么希望?

---

① 纳西族从前的习惯是老大掌家权,分家时,老二无继承权。

纳西古歌三首
Three Old Folk Songs of the Naxi

From them I feel no warmth and love.①

Treating me like an unrelated outsider,
They are the most selfish family I have seen.

Sending me, like a deserted animal, to serve
In the army without a second thought.

And turning me in as the whipping boy
For the sins they have committed.

Why would I not be saddened by
What I suffered as the second son?

The second son lives inferior to the cattle,
And the second son lives more poorly than even a daughter.

A few years at most endured, the daughter
Might inherit what her parents-in-law have left.

Yet what else is left for
The second son in the family?

---

① In the Naxi family long ago, it was always the eldest who would have the say in the family, and the second child would inherit nothing.

"当囡的还能碰上个好丈夫，
两人相好，夫妻俩也过得欢畅！

"可是当次子的啊！
一生还有什么希望！"

女：
"不要这么讲！不要这么讲！
当女的苦，你要我数哪样？

"当我一来到人世
就有九个太阳，九个月亮——

"九个太阳啊，
烤得我没处藏，

"九个月亮啊，
冻得我好似筛糠。

"我不能熬到当婆婆，
爹妈手下活不长。

"要碰上个好丈夫啊，
除了正午你能看到月亮。

纳西古歌三首
Three Old Folk Songs of the Naxi

Her beloved the daughter might meet one day,
Living happily ever after.

Yet what else is left for
The second son in the family!"

Female:
"My sufferings if you know well,
You would talk not like that!

What I suffered since the day I was born
Resembled nine suns and nine moons.

Nowhere to be found to hide from
The extreme heat of nine suns.

Shivering like chaff being sifted in the
Cold of the night with nine moons.

The day of becoming someone's mother-in-law
Might be far from reach considering how my parents treated me.

And the chance of meeting the right person
Was as slim as seeing the moon at noon.

"我在娘肚里就许了人家,①
爹妈也不管我怎样——

"男家送来一包东门②的砂糖,
爹妈就笑了;

"男家送来一坛家酿的米酒,
爹妈就请媒人坐上席了;

"男家送来几斗永胜的米,
爹妈就说话了;

"男家送来一对大理的银镯子,
爹妈就把囡卖了。

"我一生就还这一包糖的债了,
我一生就还这一坛酒的债了。

"我一生就还这几斗米的债了,
我一生就还这对银镯子的债了。

---

① 从前纳西族多指腹为婚。
② 东门,是指丽江的东门。

纳西古歌三首
Three Old Folk Songs of the Naxi

My feelings parents cared not about at all,
And betrothed me to some stranger before my birth①.

A bag of East Gate② sugar from my would-be husband
Won the favor and smile of my parents;

Homemade rice wine from my would-be husband
Won the invitation of the matchmaker to our house;

Some Yongsheng rice from my would-be husband
Won the trust and promise of my parents;

A pair of Dali silver bracelets from my would-be husband
Finally contributed to the marriage between me and him.

A bag of sugar I will devote my lifetime to pay back,
A jar of rice wine I will devote my lifetime to pay back.

A few buckets of rice I will devote my lifetime to pay back,
And a pair of silver bracelets I will devote my lifetime to pay back.

---

① It means an old practice of marriage betrothed before birth for the Naxi in the past.
② East Gate of Lijiang.

"唉,爹妈把我卖了,
只有更苦的命在前面等我;

"爹妈把我卖了,
我还不知道那个男人怎样,

"是猫,还是狗?
是人的模样?是狼的心肠?

"我怎能嫁给他呀,
嫁到那个荒凉的地方!

"那家住在荒山上,
茨蓬漫山地长,

"山坡小得像指头,
地方大不过手掌。

"要下力,没地方下手,
要放羊,没有牧场。

"我怎么能嫁给他呀,
嫁给一个不相识的男子汉!

纳西古歌三首
Three Old Folk Songs of the Naxi

A stranger, alas, my parents cruelly sold me to,
And waiting ahead is something unknown and miserable.

A stranger, alas, my parents cruelly sold me to,
And waiting ahead is someone I know not.

His appearance I have no sense of,
And his character too I barely understand.

How can I, alas, marry a stranger from
Somewhere remote and deserted?

A barren mountain he comes from,
Where thorns grow all over.

As small as a thumb is the small hill,
And where he lives is no bigger than a palm.

Nowhere can be found to do farm work,
Let alone a meadow for the sheep.

How can I, alas, marry him,
Some stranger I have never met before?

"他一定是个恶毒的人,
不然,为什么我没降生就差媒人来到门上!

"他一定是个恶毒的人呀,
一双镯子就想买头牛到他家去呀!

"一对镯子买不到一头牛啊,
卖了我的,却是爹娘!

男:
"你为什么流泪,
你为什么不把话讲。

"我以后要对你有半点不好,
我就没有好下场!

"相信我吧,姑娘!
"随我走吧,姑娘!"

女:
"我不是不愿跟你去,
我流泪不是悲伤。

"蜜蜂虽然飞不高,

纳西古歌三首
Three Old Folk Songs of the Naxi

A vicious man, alas, he must be, otherwise,
A matchmaker he would not send before my birth!

A vicious man, alas, he must be, otherwise,
A pair of bracelets he would not trade me for!

Impossible is it to trade one cow for a pair of bracelet,
Yet saying yes to the deal of marriage were my birth parents!"

Male:
"Pour out your sufferings please, fair maiden,
Rather than weep and say nothing.

No good end comes, I swear, if
I fail to keep what I promised.

You have my word, my dear maiden!
Come with me, please, my dear maiden!"

Female:
"No one knows how much I want to be with you,
And the tears I shed are by no means out of sadness.

Though the honey bees fly not high,

可到过每个开花的地方；

"我看过的人也不少，
没一个像你这样好心肠。

"娘生我，没你这样对我好，
爹养我，没你这样对我好。

"年轻人，我相信你，
跟着你走，我就会平安。

"我永远不会离开你，
像蜜蜂永远不离开鲜花，

"蜂子离开花不酿蜜，
花离开蜜蜂不开花。"

男：

"姑娘，我相信你说的都是真话，
你说的，也正是我心里的话。"

女：

"可是，假若有一天风霜逼我俩分离，
我俩又有什么办法？"

纳西古歌三首
Three Old Folk Songs of the Naxi

Every blossom they have visited.

Quite a few people I have met,
Yet you are the first with such a kind heart.

My mother, giving me life though, compares not with you,
My father, bringing me up though, compares not with you either.

I have faith in you, my dear lad,
With you I would end up happily ever after.

For good I will leave you not,
Like bees live not without flowers.

Bees make not honey without flowers,
And flowers blossom not without bees."

Male:
"I do believe, my maiden, what you said,
Which is just what I hold in my mind."

Female:
"Yet we could do nothing I am afraid,
If the cruel reality separates us one day."

男：

"有一天风霜逼我们分离，
我们就同焚在一个炉里变成火花。

"变成一缕云烟升在天上，
或者变成一片红霞。

"姑娘，跟着我什么都不怕，
你也不要胡思乱想吧！"

女：

"年轻人，不是我胡思乱想，
有水的地方，就有风浪。

"好花是由好种栽出来，
好树是由好枝接出来；

"年轻人，我既然这样爱你，
就不能不为我俩以后的日子着想。

"不然，风波要突然袭来，
我就无法承担。"

纳西古歌三首
Three Old Folk Songs of the Naxi

Male:

"If life setbacks do separate us one day,

Ashes we would rather burn ourselves into.

Turning at last, into a wisp of smoke,

Or the magnificent sunset glow.

Do not be pessimistic about our future,

With me you have nothing to be afraid of!"

Female:

"My consideration, lad, comes for a reason,

Disputes appear as long as people exist.

Quality seeds cultivate fine flowers,

And the best trees grow out of nice branches.

Feelings of love I have shown to you, my lad,

So our future I shall take into consideration.

Trouble, otherwise, coming all of a sudden,

Would be out of my capability to handle."

男：

"只要我俩同心，
任何风浪都能抵挡。

"姑娘啊，我的姑娘，
你怎么不能摆脱这些恼人的思想？"

女：

"年轻人，我活过的日子都是这样，
没有一步走得顺当。

"我从没想到幸福会来到我头上，
我真怕我俩的幸福不会长。

"假若你被抓去一定回不来，
我看你，只有在有星星的早上——

"在黄铜盆里的凉水里，
我洗脸，你的影子映在水上；

"水里的影子，看不清人，
你的样子，只能让我想。

"如果你被抓去，

纳西古歌三首
Three Old Folk Songs of the Naxi

Male:

"As long as we have faith in each other,
Nothing can block our way ahead.

Could you please, my dear maiden,
Rid yourself of the unnecessary worries?"

Female:

"The bumpy road I have grown accustomed to,
And dare not to expect any miracles.

Never did I expect the approaching of happiness,
Nor should I be unconcerned about the happy life with you.

You must return not if caught, then
I will meet you only on the mornings with stars!

Your reflection, then, is shown from
The yellow brass basin while I am washing;

Yet unclear is the water reflection,
Your appearance I have only to look back on.

A butterfly I would turn into in the daytime

我白天要变成蝴蝶去找你;

"如果你被抓去,
我晚上要变成萤火虫去找你。

"哥,你不能被抓去啊,
请你留在我身旁。"

男:
"抓去了,我也是死,
没抓去,我还是死,

"我要死,也不去当替死鬼,
我要死,也死在你身旁。

"世上没一片叶子不想发绿,
天上的星星没一颗不想发光——

"放心吧,我的姑娘,
爱你的人不会离开你身旁。"

女:
"哦,哥哥,我的情郎,
现在不是你发誓的时光。

纳西古歌三首
Three Old Folk Songs of the Naxi

Looking for you if you get caught soon;

A glowworm I would turn into at night
Looking for you if you get caught soon.

Please, alas, do not get caught.
How I wish we could stay together."

Male:
"I will end up dead if caught,
Otherwise waiting ahead is the same destiny.

I would rather die than be a whipping man,
I would rather die by your side if I have to.

No leaf in the world wants not to turn green,
And stars in the sky all expect to glow.

The last thing, dear maiden, I would do
Is to leave you behind in this world."

Female:
"My dear brother, alas, my dear lad,
The time of promising is not yet now.

"锦竹生根在寒冷的山头,
牡丹开在温暖的地方——

"苦命人和苦命人在一起,
那还有什么话讲!"

男:
"快走!快走,姑娘,
你听,是什么人在喧嚷!"

女:
"那是追赶你的人,
那是来抓你的人。

"你快跑吧,
跑到你要去的地方!"

男:
"可是你哩?可是你哩?
我不能把你送给他们啊,姑娘!"

女:
"我留在这里,他们只能抓一个,

纳西古歌三首
Three Old Folk Songs of the Naxi

A cold mountain top finds roots of bamboo,
And peony blossoms in the warm place.

Your honesty is the last thing I should doubt,
Since we share the same destiny together."

Male:
"Hurry up and go, my dear maiden,
I hear someone following behind!

Female:
People chasing you from behind come,
People aiming to catch you come.

Hurry up and escape to where
You are meant to be!"

Male:
"Yet impossible is it to leave you behind,
And leave you to their evil clutches! My maiden!"

Female:
"Leave you alone they will if I stay,

我跟着你走,他们要抓一双。

"抓住你,他们要你死,
逃走,你还有活命的地方!

"抓住你,只有去当冤魂,
我留在这里,还能把风暴抵挡。

"快走吧,年轻人,
他们就要追上来了……"

……

五

"去吧,我们去寻那美丽的世界,
它在庄严的雪山上。

"那里有三个水晶般的雪岩,
多是玛瑙血石。

"奇花宝树遍山顶,
四季常青的绿叶总遮着阳光。

纳西古歌三首
Three Old Folk Songs of the Naxi

Yet if we run we will both get caught.

You will end up dead if caught,
Yet there is still hope to live if you run!

A wandering ghost you might become if caught,
So I would rather stay to meet the misfortune.

Hurry up and run, my lad,
Otherwise, they might catch up…"

…

V

"Let's look for the beautiful world
Which lies in the solemn snow mountain.

There we can find three crystal-like snow rocks,
Among most of which resemble agate stones.

The mountain top dotted with exquisite flowers and rare trees,
And sunlight sheltered from the evergreen leaves.

"右面流下来一条金水,
左面的河里有银子流淌。

"土地不耕就松了,
不播种就长了绿苗。

"你渴了,喝口金银水,
你不高兴了,看着遍地的花草。

"金花开在山南,
银花开在山北。

"鲜花上的鸟像吹笛子一样叫,
鲜花上的蜜蜂嚷得像口弦一样响。

"琉璃雪石是我俩的卧床,
雉鸡当报晓的晨鸡。

"银狐是我们的看家狗,
驯虎为我们当马骑,

"玉鹿为我们当耕牛,
白云为我们做上天的阶梯,

纳西古歌三首
Three Old Folk Songs of the Naxi

The stream on the right side flows gold in the water,
And on the left flows silver in the water.

Without ploughing, the soil becomes loose,
And without seeding, out of it grows sprouts.

To quench thirst we drink golden and silver water,
And to cheer us up we appreciate flowers and plants.

On the south mountain blossom golden flowers,
And on the north silver blossoms in full bloom.

Birds staying on flowers sing like flute playing, and
Bees collecting honey are as noisy as the sound of a jaw harp.

Crystal-like snow rock we sleep on,
And a pheasant heralds the break of day for us.

Guarding the house is the silver fox,
And the tiger is tamed to ride.

Ploughing has been done by the Jade Deer,
And via clouds we can reach the sky.

"山上还有拉萨的大黑石，
可以站在上面四周瞭望。

"去吧，我们去那个地方，
去到那个美丽的天堂。

"我们永远相亲相爱，
在那一个地方……"

纳西古歌三首
Three Old Folk Songs of the Naxi

On the mountain finds Lhasa's gigantic black rock

Which we can stand on to overlook the scene below.

Go, let us go to that place,

To the beautiful heaven on earth.

There once we arrive,

Nothing could part us forever…"

About the Translator

Chen Jinjin pursued her master's degree at Shanghai International Studies University, majoring in translation studies. Now she works in the School of Foreign Languages and Literature of Yunnan Normal University. Her research area covers corpus translation studies and ethnic classics translation studies. She is the Principal Investigator of "English Translation Studies of Minority Classics from the Perspective of Corpus Linguistics", a project sponsored by Yunnan Provincial Department of Education. Chen Jinjin has participated in the translation of *The Diary of Dong Haoyun*, UN documents and national publicity films.